Mates, Dates & Great Escapes

Also available by Cathy Hopkins

The MATES, DATES series

1. Mates, Dates and Inflatable Bras
2. Mates, Dates and Cosmic Kisses
3. Mates, Dates and Portobello Princesses
4. Mates, Dates and Sleepover Secrets
5. Mates, Dates and Sole Survivors
6. Mates, Dates and Mad Mistakes
7. Mates, Dates and Pulling Power
8. Mates, Dates and Tempting Trouble
9. Mates, Dates and Great Escapes
10. Mates, Dates and Chocolate Cheats
11. Mates, Dates and Diamond Destiny
12. Mates, Dates and Sizzling Summers

Companion Books:
Mates, Dates Guide to Life
Mates, Dates and You
Mates, Dates Journal

The TRUTH, DARE, KISS OR PROMISE series

1. White Lies and Barefaced Truths
2. Pop Princess
3. Teen Queens and Has-Beens
4. Starstruck
5. Double Dare
6. Midsummer Meltdown
7. Love Lottery
8. All Mates Together

The CINNAMON GIRL series

1. This Way to Paradise
2. Starting Over

Cathy Hopkins

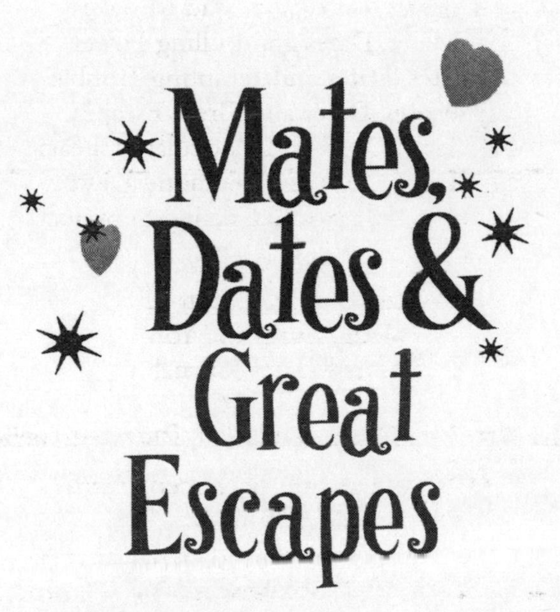

PICCADILLY PRESS • LONDON

Thanks to Brenda Gardner, Yasemin Uçar and the ever fab team at Piccadilly. Also to Rosemary Bromley at Juvenilia. And to Steve Lovering for being such a patient listening ear when working out outlines, and for accompanying me to Florence to research the locations in the book (although I don't think he minded too much). Also to Laura Denham for good advice for overcoming fear of flying. And to Scott Brenman, Edward Jeffrey, Olivia McDonnell, Alice Elwes and Natalie Reeves for giving me the low-down on school trips from a teen's point of view. And big thanks to all the lovely readers out there who buy the books and send me their letters and e-mails.

First published in Great Britain in 2004
by Piccadilly Press Ltd.,
5 Castle Road, London NW1 8PR

This edition published 2007.

A catalogue record for this book is available from the British Library

ISBN: 978 1 85340 935 6 (trade paperback)

1 3 5 7 9 10 8 6 4 2

Printed in the UK by CPI Bookmarque, Croydon, CR0 4TD
Typeset by Textype Typesetters
Cover design by Simon Davis

Set in 11.5pt Bembo and Lush

Chapter 1

Turning Scarlet

A light above the surgery door flashed on and a few people in the waiting room looked up expectantly.

'Mrs Harper,' called the nurse at the reception desk. 'Go on through.'

A blonde lady who had been sitting next to us got up and made her way through to the surgery.

'Let's get out of here, Lucy,' said Nesta. 'I thought you were joking.'

'Yeah. Seems a bit drastic to me,' said TJ looking about nervously. 'Giving blood is not my idea of a fun way to spend Saturday morning.'

'I know, but hey, drastic situation, drastic measures,' I said. 'And I'm not asking any of you to do it. I think it's a good idea regardless of my problem and why I first suggested coming here. It may save a life.'

Izzie pointed at a poster on the wall. 'Yeah,' she said, 'it's a way of giving something back to the community. Says there that only six per cent of people donate blood.'

Nesta put her hands into the prayer position. 'St Lucy and St Izzie, out to save the world. No way I'm doing it. Can't we just put a quid in the donation box instead?'

We were sitting in the waiting room at the blood donor clinic. I'd seen the poster outside the Tube on the way home from school last night and dragged my mates in here this morning. *Save a Life by Donating Blood*, the poster read. Save my life, I thought as I had a brainwave. It could be the answer to the curse that follows me everywhere I go. Blushing. Giving blood could be the solution. One pint less, one pint less to blush with. The girls thought I'd gone barking mad and laughed their heads off when I told them. I guess it was a bit bonkers to think that it would solve my blushing problem, but I got to thinking that even if it was a daft idea, giving blood can save a life (as the poster said), so no harm done and I'd manage to do a good deed in the bargain.

'And I don't think blushing is a problem,' said TJ. 'I think it's sweet when you turn pink.'

Yeah right, I thought. I know different. It makes me look like a kid and it's embarrassing and a half. I blush so easily at the maddest things. Like if anyone says *any* word with the slightest sexual connotation, I turn purple. Like in biology last Wednesday, we were doing the reproductive behaviour of frogs. Frogs! How unsexy are they? But in the course of the lesson, our teacher, Miss Aspinall, said reproductive organs and, baboom, I turned scarlet. I *hate* it. It's not like I'm a prude or even really embarrassed, but some out of control part of me has decided that if I hear a sexual word or I'm talking to a boy I fancy, blood will flood to my face. It's weird – if I'm in the dark and no one's looking at me, I'm fine. I can hear anything, watch anything, the rudest most disgusting thing, and I know I won't blush, but, if the lights are up or people are looking at me, I turn pink at anything. Of course, my brother Lal is well aware of the fact and uses any excuse to get me going. Like last night he said, 'Pubic hair', turned to me and waited with a great stupid grin on his face. I could have thumped him. Course, I turned red on cue. How pathetic is that? I can't control it. No *way* am I embarrassed by pubic hair. Everybody gets it. But say the words and look me in the eye and off I go. Pink, red, scarlet. Stupid, stupid, stupid.

'Next,' called the nurse at the reception desk.

I stood up and walked towards her.

'Name?' she asked.

'Lucy Lovering.'

'Age?'

'Fourteen. Fifteen in May.'

The nurse peered over her glasses. 'Not old enough,' she said and looked beyond me at the waiting queue. 'Next.'

Not old enough. Story of my life, I thought as I went back to join the others. Nesta, Izzie and TJ. My mates. My mates that are all the same age as me, but look like they're eighteen, whereas I look like I only just crawled out of junior school. Nesta's five foot seven, TJ's five foot seven and Izzie has had a spurt of growing recently and is the tallest of all of us at five foot eight. Me, I've had my own growing spurt too, bringing me up to the grand height of five feet. Woopedoop. Not. It causes no end of trouble, like if we ever want to go and see an adult film. They all sail in, no questions asked at the cinema ticket counter, then they get to me and it's no go. Last time we tried it, Izzie was ahead of me in the queue. 'Can't let your little sister through,' the sales person said to Izzie and everyone in the foyer turned and stared at me. I could have died, and went bright red as usual. Well, my mates might look older than me, taller than me, they might be ahead of the game in many areas, but there's one major part of growing up where I may just pip them all to the post.

Blushing Tips

Wear pale make-up, although this can also make you look ill. *Nesta*

Only go out in the dark (bit limiting, but it is an option). *Lucy*

What you resist persists, so if you stop fighting it and even announce when it's going to happen – 'I'm going to go red' – it will probably go away. *Izzie*

Um. Wear very bright red lipstick; that way when you blush, your face will match your lips. OK. Not my best idea. I dunno. I think it's sweet when people blush. *TJ*

P.S.: Donating blood isn't going to help one bit. *Dr Watts (TJ's mum)*

Chapter 2

Be Prepared

We were back at Izzie's when I brought the subject up. We were up in her bedroom and she was on the internet on her favourite astrology site, downloading our horoscopes for February.

'Hey Nesta, this is true,' said Izzie scanning the print out of Leo. 'Says you're in for some foreign travel.'

'And for you and TJ,' said Nesta. 'Our school trip to Florence.'

'I know. I can't wait,' said Izzie. 'Mum's been plying me with books about the place. She's all for me getting a bit of culture smulture – art galleries, taking in the talent of centuries gone by.'

'I was thinking about a different kind of talent,' said Nesta, 'like all those gorgeous Italian boys. I've been brushing up on my Italian so I'll be able to chat to them in their language.'

'And you could all pass as Italians,' I said. Unlike me with my short blond hair, Nesta, TJ and Izzie have got long dark hair. I could just see them swanning through the streets of Florence, looking cool in big black sunglasses. 'The local boys won't know what's hit them.'

'I thought you'd be through with Italian boys after he who shall not be named,' said Izzie.

Nesta flicked her hair back. 'You mean Luke? He was a minor blip. Not all boys are like him.'

I noticed that TJ looked uncomfortable and was staring at the floor. Luke De Biasi. Love rat extraordinaire and the first boy to almost split us up as friends. He was going out with Nesta, then declared undying passion for TJ, who I think did genuinely fall in love with him. It got a bit messy for a time. Nesta was devastated; TJ was confused as hell. I took sides with Nesta and Izzie took sides with TJ. It was horrible. In the end, we all decided that losing our friendship over a boy, a boy who told lies no less, wasn't worth it and he got dumped. I think it affected TJ more than she lets on though. I think she really thought that Luke was her soulmate. Nesta's not a soulmate kind of girl. She collects boys' hearts like other girls collect handbags. She wants to experience as many as possible she says and, with her stunning exotic looks (she's half-Italian, half-Jamaican), she's never short of admirers.

'What does mine say?' asked TJ.

Izzie looked at the screen. 'Hhmmm. Sagittarius. New horizons will open up to you.'

'It will be my first time in Italy, so I guess that counts as a new horizon,' she said.

Izzie looked at me sympathetically. 'I wish you were coming Luce,' she said.

'Yeah,' said TJ. 'Isn't there any way? I heard there are a couple of places left. Apparently Alice Riley and Georgia Watson have dropped out.'

I shook my head. 'No chance. My family can't afford a bus ride to Scunthorpe at the moment, never mind a trip to Italy. What does my horoscope say, Iz?'

Izzie punched in a few keys and brought up the horoscope for Gemini. 'Oh. Hhmm. Sounds ambiguous. Something you have been considering for a time is about to come to a head and you have to decide which way you want to play it. Dunno. What do you think that means?'

'Tony,' I said.

I've been dating Nesta's older brother on and off for a while now, and lately we've settled into being a proper couple. Regular dates. Regular phone calls. Regular snogging sessions on the sofa when our parents are out. I first saw him crossing the road in Highgate outside his school. Cute, dark, wide gorgeous mouth. It was love at first sight. The reason I wouldn't let things get serious before now was because he always wanted to take things further – further in the sense of from the sitting room and in to the bedroom. I didn't feel ready, plus he may be the love of my life, but I'm not blind. He can get any girl he wants and he likes a challenge. I've been a challenge as I've been fending him off. It wasn't my intention to get so involved at this stage in my life. I wanted to be like Nesta and play the field a bit. I'm not fifteen yet and thought there would be plenty of time for serious relationships later, but you can't help who you fall in love with. Along came Tony and it all started happening. Still is all happening. But he's three years older than me; he wants to sleep with me and he's not going to wait forever.

'What do you mean? Tony?' asked Nesta.

'Well, I do really really like him, so I'm thinking about going to number ten.'

TJ looked up from one of Izzie's books that she had her nose in. 'Number ten?' she asked. 'You're going to see the Prime Minister with Tony?'

I laughed. Sometimes I think TJ is on another planet. 'No, dummy. As in go all the way.'

'All the way? Wow,' said Nesta. 'Woah.'

Izzie turned away from her computer. 'This is a bit sudden,' she said. 'Are you sure?'

'Yes. No. I mean, why not? And it's not really sudden. I've been thinking about it a lot. You have to do it sometime and I've known Tony a long time now and we really do like each other . . .'

'Yeah, but you always said you didn't want to rush things,' said Izzie.

'But we haven't,' I protested. 'We've been going together for ages now. So why not do what he wants? I have to get it over with sometime.'

'Yeah, but with *Tony*?' said Nesta, making a disgusted face.

'And you make it sound like a chore,' said Izzie, 'saying you have to do it sometime. Like it's on a must do list. Must clean bedroom, must do homework, must have sex with boyfriend.'

I sighed. I couldn't deny that it did feel a bit like that. Like an exam looming in the future. I can't say I was looking forward to it that much, as I don't know if I'll be any good at it. It was bad enough worrying if I was an OK kisser, but everybody has to do it sooner or later so why not with someone I like as much as Tony?

'When?' asked TJ.

'I don't know. I haven't totally decided, I mean . . . I haven't even told him that I'm thinking about it.'

'Where?' asked Izzie.

'Where? I don't know. Give me a break. I told you, I haven't decided definitely. I wanted to talk to you guys first.'

'Well I don't think you should,' said Nesta. 'You're not even fifteen yet, and he's eighteen.'

'Yeah, but if she is thinking about it,' said Izzie turning to Nesta, 'she has to be ready. Like she doesn't want her mum finding her and lover boy in the nudie pants on the sitting room sofa. She'd have a fit.'

'Er, excuse me,' I said. 'I am in the room here.'

Izzie turned back to me. 'But seriously, Lucy,' she said. 'Have you really thought this through?'

'Yes and no. The time and the place maybe not, but with love how can you plan it? Surely the right moment will present itself. We'll just know it and if we're in a place where it's OK, then . . .'

Nesta folded her arms. 'No,' she said. 'You're too young.'

Izzie snorted. 'You sound like my mum,' she said, then put on a voice like the queen. 'Lucy Lovering. You're *far* too young.'

'Yeah, but Lucy, you are,' said Nesta. 'I read somewhere that the average age that most people lose their virginity is seventeen.'

'So?' I said. 'Who wants to be average? Anyway, *I* read in one of mum's magazines that a quarter of teenagers have lost their virginity by the time they're fifteen. So there. I think you're just saying I shouldn't because you want to be the first.'

'Am not. I don't want to do it until I've been with someone for ages and I really, really love them.'

'But I do love Tony.'

'I agree with Nesta,' said Izzie. 'Really Luce, you're not old enough. I think you're doing it just to keep him happy.'

I sighed. 'Here we go again. I'm so sick of hearing that, not old enough. It's the story of my life. Not old enough. Not old enough. Why shouldn't I do it? Why not? It's not like I haven't known Tony for ages and why shouldn't I want to make him happy? He does loads of things for me . . .'

'Condoms,' interrupted TJ.

'What about them?' I asked.

'You'll need them if you do it. Have you got any?'

'No. Why?'

'D'oh. Safe sex, dummy, and you need protection from STDs.'

'What are they?' I asked.

'Sexually transmitted diseases,' said TJ. She's our local medical expert. Both her parents are doctors, so she picks up loads of information about diseases and stuff. 'My mum said that loads of people she sees at her surgery who have had unprotected sex get chlamydia.'

'What's chlamydia?' I asked. 'Sounds like a posh girl's name – like Lady Chlamydia Armstrong Wotnot.'

TJ laughed. 'Yeah, but it's not a name. It's a disease which is very common, apparently has few side effects so many people don't even realise that they've got it, but if untreated it can lead to infertility.'

'Chlamydia, condoms, STDs, unwanted pregnancies,' I said. 'What happened to *romance*?'

Nesta sighed. 'See,' she said. 'Head in the clouds.'

'Yeah. You have to be responsible,' said TJ. 'You don't want to get pregnant.'

'Since when did you lot become such . . . such killjoys?' I asked, as the rosy glow around my fantasy began to fade.

'We're not being killjoys,' said Nesta. 'We're your mates. We're looking out for you.

'Hmf. Feels more like you're ganging up on me.'

'No, we're not,' said Izzie. 'It's just best to be prepared. To know what you're getting into. Tell you what, let's look condoms up on the internet. I'll go into one of the search engines.'

She pressed a few keys and, a moment later, a whole list of website addresses came up. After a few seconds, she started laughing.

'Ohmi*god*! You can get anything and everything on here. Here. Here's the one for you! I'll read it,' said Izzie as she studied her screen. '*Surprise your partner and add a new dimension to your love life with a glow-in-the-dark condom. It will make it a night to remember.*'

We all cracked up. The image of Tony wearing a glow-in-the-dark condom was hysterical.

'There's loads more,' said Izzie as she scrolled down her computer screen. 'Ohmi*god*! I never realised there were so many types!'

'What like, small, medium and liar?' I asked.

'All sorts . . .' Izzie said, laughing, as we crowded round the computer to have a better look.

We were so busy scanning the pages and laughing our heads off at all the types that came up that we didn't notice that the door had opened and Izzie's mum had come in.

'What's so funny?' she asked.

Izzie almost jumped out of her skin.

'*Mum*! I've *told* you to knock!' she said as she quickly closed the site, went back to her desktop and assumed her best innocent look.

As Mrs Foster eyed us suspiciously, I felt myself starting to blush and prayed that it wouldn't give the game away. Mrs Foster can be really intimidating when she wants to be. She's so different to my mum, who is easy-going and looks like an old hippie. Mrs Foster looks like a proper grown-up, always in high heels and immaculate clothes, never a hair out of place.

'What could you possibly be doing that you wouldn't want me to know about?' Mrs Foster asked, lifting her nose to the air and sniffing. 'You haven't been smoking in here, have you?'

'Mum,' groaned Izzie. 'I don't smoke. Won't smoke. Give me a break.'

Mrs Foster shrugged. 'Ah well. I'm going to the supermarket and wanted to know if any of you were here for a late lunch or early supper?'

'No thanks,' chorused Nesta, TJ and I.

'No,' said Izzie, looking pointedly at me. 'We've got some very important window shopping to do.'

'What for?' asked Mrs Foster. 'Italy?'

Izzie tapped the side of her nose. 'Something we learned from the Girl Guides,' she said. 'You know their motto: Be prepared.'

That set us all off laughing again.

Mrs Foster looked mystified. 'Right,' she said. 'Suit yourselves.'

Girl Guides motto: Be prepared.

Chapter 3

The Pros and Cons of Toothpaste

First stop was a pharmacy in East Finchley to get some nail polish remover for Izzie.

'Seriously though,' said TJ, as we made our way up the High Street, 'you do have to think about birth control. You can't expect the boy to take all the responsibility.'

'I guess,' I said. I was still feeling like the girls had put a major dampener on my mood. Part of me could see that they were right – I hadn't really thought it through properly, but another part felt like they just didn't want me to be the first to do something for once.

'I guess it wouldn't hurt to check out what they sell in the chemist's,' I said. 'As you said, be prepared, and I certainly can't buy them off the internet.'

'OK,' said Izzie. 'Where do you want to look? The pharmacists in Cootes are really nice. I'm sure they'll be very helpful.'

'No way,' I said. 'My mum shops there. I can just imagine her popping in for shampoo or something and them letting on that her dear virginal daughter had just been in looking at condoms.'

'There are loads of other chemists,' said TJ. 'There's one right at the end of the High Street. That's usually pretty quiet and we wouldn't want anyone seeing us checking out the selection.'

We made our way up to the last row of shops and hovered outside the chemist's, pretending that we were looking at the window display, that is until Izzie pointed out that we were all staring at a promotion advertising ointment for piles.

'Hhhmmm. Fascinating, not,' she said.

'Nesta, please will you go in and check them out for me?' I asked. 'The shop assistant will take one look at me and come out with the you're-not-old-enough line.'

'But you're not buying any,' said Izzie.

'Even so,' I said. 'I can't bear to hear that you're-not-old-enough line once more, and you do look the most grown-up out of all of us.'

'Sure I'll look for you,' said Nesta. 'I'll pretend that I'm a character in a film and I'm about to go away with my lover on a romantic weekend to Paris.'

'Whatever,' I said. I was used to Nesta acting out scenes from films in her head. She wants to be an actress when she leaves school and believes in practising at every given moment. 'The rest of us can come in with you and look at the make-up or something.'

We shuffled our way into the shop and, while the assistant was serving a customer, we scoured the shelves.

'Over there,' said Izzie after a few minutes, 'to the left of the cash till.'

We waited until the customer left and the shop became empty, then Nesta straightened herself up as tall as she could and walked over to the cash till. She looked at the condoms on display, then came over to us at the other side of the shop.

'They have all sorts: gossamer, extra lubricated, extra safe, ribbed, sheer . . .'

I pulled a face. 'They sound horrible. Like old ladies' tights.'

'And they come in packs of three or twelve.'

I felt myself turning pink. '*Twelve?* Gimme a break. I wonder how much they cost. The three-pack, I mean. They've probably got a price written on them or you could ask the assistant.'

'OK,' said Nesta and made her way back to the counter. She was just about to pick up a pack, when the shop door bell binged to indicate another customer had come in. Nesta's face was a picture. Her jaw fell open when she saw who the customer was and she quickly withdrew her hand from the condoms. At the back of the shop, Izzie, TJ and I darted behind a large display of spectacles and sunglasses.

'Mrs *Allen*!' said Nesta, putting on a big cheesy grin. 'What a lovely surprise. Um, er, yes, menthol or whitener? It's always such a hard decision, don't you think?'

She picked up a tube of toothpaste and held it in front of our headmistress's face. Mrs Allen looked at her quizzically.

'Yes, Nesta, I suppose it is,' she said, picking up a packet of aspirin. 'Now while you debate the pros and cons of toothpaste, do you mind if I go ahead of you? I'm in a bit of a hurry.'

'Oh no, I mean, yes, please, go ahead,' stuttered Nesta, losing her cool for a moment and glancing back at us. 'I've got to get a few things.'

She raced back to our side of the shop and looked mystified when she couldn't see us.

Mrs Allen paid for her purchases and headed for the door. 'Behind the spectacle counter,' she said whilst looking straight ahead.

'What? Who?' asked Nesta, trying her best to look wide-eyed and innocent.

'Your mates,' said Mrs Allen. 'Lucy Lovering, Izzie Foster and Theresa Watts. For some reason, they're cowering behind the sunglasses stand.'

Nesta turned and looked in the direction of the spectacle display. Izzie, who had put on a large, black pair of sunglasses, poked her head out and gave Mrs Allen a half-hearted wave as she went out of the door.

'I swear she didn't even glance in our direction,' said Izzie as Nesta raced over to join us. 'It must be a job requirement for being a headmistress. Eyes in the back of your head.'

Nesta went and peered out of the window and down the High Street. 'She's gone into the hairdresser's,' she said. 'Coast clear.'

'Can I help you girls with anything?' called the shop assistant, who by now was eyeing us suspiciously.

'Um, yes. Just getting some make-up remover pads,' Nesta called back.

She was about to make her way back to the counter again when, once more, the door chinked that there was another customer.

'Not our day is it?' said Izzie, as we all darted back behind the spectacle display.

'No,' I said, then indicated the spectacles on sale. 'We can't be seen to make spectacles of ourselves.'

TJ started giggling, then and that set me off, then Izzie.

'Keep it together, you guys,' hushed Nesta.

'Who is it?' I asked. 'Can you see who came in? Best check it's not Mrs Allen back for some eye drops for her extra set of eyes or something.'

Nesta poked her head round the corner of the display. 'Ohmigod, get back,' she said. 'It's Candice Carter.'

'Oh *no,*' I groaned. Candice is a mate in our year, but she's one of the biggest gossips in the school. Tell her anything and it spreads like Asian flu.

'She's probably come in for more of that colour she puts on her hair,' said Izzie. Candice was always experimenting with her hair colour. Lately it had been a bright raspberry red.

'No. No, I don't think so, as the hair colour is at the front of the shop,' said Nesta. 'She's . . . oh, I think she may be buying condoms – she looks pretty nervous. She's looking round to check that no one's watching.'

We all stayed very still while Nesta tried to see what was going on.

'Oh Lord,' she said after a few minutes. 'You'll never guess what she's bought.'

'What?' I asked, as at last the door chinked that Candice had gone.

'A pregnancy test!' said Nesta.

'You're kidding,' said Izzie. 'Candice?'

'Ohmigod,' I said. 'I wonder if she is. Pregnant, that is. She has been going with Elliot, a boy from Wood Green High, for months now. I wonder if they've done it.'

'I'd say most definitely from the look of things,' said Nesta.

We stared at each other in silence for a few moments.

'Girls,' called the shop assistant suddenly appearing round the corner of the display, 'have you made your minds up yet? Do you want to buy something or not?'

Nesta looked at me and raised an eyebrow. 'Lucy?'

'Yes,' I said. 'Um, do you sell chastity belts?'

Position of Headmistress: Only those with
an extra set of eyes need apply.

Chapter 4

Mrs Finkelstein

I was on the Jerry Springer *show, trying to balance my three giant babies on my knees but wasn't succeeding, and one of them kept slipping down on to the floor. I looked terrible. Haggard, pale and spotty with bedraggled, unwashed hair.*

'What are the babies' names?' asked Jerry.

'Nesta, Izzie and TJ,' I sobbed. 'I named them after my mates at school.'

'Even though the babies are boys?' asked Jerry.

I nodded sadly.

'And when exactly did you turn to drink, Lucy?' asked Jerry.

'When the father of my babies deserted me for a Hollywood starlet and left me living in a dustbin,' I whispered and the studio audience gasped in horror.

'Well, tonight, we're going to hear from Tony,' said Jerry. 'He's been waiting backstage to tell his side of the story. Come on out, Tony.'

Tony appeared at the side of the stage and the audience booed loudly. He looked gorgeous, clean, radiant, at his most handsome. I began to hit him round the head with one of the babies, which had now turned into a pillow.

'Lucy,' said Jerry. His voice sounded strange. Feminine. 'Lucy . . .'

'Wha . . .?' I opened my eyes to find Mum leaning over me.

'Come on, love, get a move on. It's time to get up,' she said. 'Bathroom's free.'

'Urggh,' I said from the depths of my duvet. I took a deep breath and willed myself to wake up properly. It took me a moment to realise that I'd been dreaming. It was such a relief to wake up and find myself safe and babyless.

'Lucy, you're miles away,' said Dad at breakfast. 'What's going on in that head of yours?'

'Oh, nothing,' I said, turning pink. I couldn't tell him about my dream. No way.

'It's not possible to think about nothing,' said Steve, my swot-box brainy brother, as he tucked into a slice of toast and peanut butter. 'I've tried. Even if your mind goes blank, you still think the thought, my mind is blank.'

'Whatever,' I said. I pushed away my half-eaten bowl of muesli and got up from the table.

'Aren't you going to finish that?' asked Mum.

I shook my head. 'Not hungry.'

'Then take an apple to school,' said Mum as she went to collect the mail that had just plopped on to the mat in the hall.

Dad looked at me kindly. 'Is something bothering you, Luce? You're very quiet this morning.'

'No, not really, that is, well . . .'

'I knew there was,' said Dad. 'So spill. What is it? You're on drugs, become a compulsive gambler? What?'

'Yeah, right.' I smiled weakly. 'No, er . . . just had a bad dream and . . . there's the school trip next month to Florence. Nesta, TJ and Izzie are going and I wish I was going with them, that's all.' That should put him off asking about my dream, I thought. I have to be careful with Mum and Dad sometimes. Both of them love to analyse dreams and they have a way of getting information out of you before you know it. Mum – because she's a counsellor and works all day getting people who don't want to talk to open up, and Dad – because he's so chilled and unjudgemental. Like Mum, he's a bit of an old hippie with his ponytail and liberal views about everything. This time however, I didn't think he'd be so liberal. Dads can come over all protective of their daughters when it comes to boys. And having triplets.

Mum sighed as she came back in with the mail. 'Did I hear you talking about the Florence trip? I am sorry you can't go with the others, Lucy, but you know how things are at the moment. Steve needs a new winter jacket, Lal needs trainers, the car insurance is due this month, the mortgage payments have just gone up, we've had a ginormous phone bill . . . It's never-ending, so I'm afraid money for school trips is out of the question.'

'I know. That's why I haven't gone on about it.'

'Our school is going on a skiing trip,' said Steve. 'I'd love to do that one of these days, years, lifetimes.'

Dad didn't say anything; he just looked at Mum, rolled his eyes and shrugged his shoulders.

Mum sat down at the head of the table and started to go through the post. 'See,' she said, holding up the wad of envelopes to us, 'nothing but bills, bills, bills.' She put the pile in front of her and sifted through until she came to one that looked like a personal letter. 'Oh, what's this one?' She opened the envelope and read. 'Oh dear,' she said after a few moments.

Dad got up and looked over her shoulder. 'What is it, love?'

Mum glanced anxiously at Lal. 'Mrs Finkelstein.'

'What?' said Lal, as Dad read the letter, then also looked in his direction. 'Whatever it is, I didn't do it.'

'It's from Mrs Finkelstein's solicitor,' said Dad.

Lal went white. 'But . . . but . . . it was *ages* ago that I broke her window. Last year. And I went and apologised. Even paid for it out of my pocket money. Remember?'

Everyone knew Mrs Finkelstein. And her house. She'd lived in the large detached one at the end of our street as far back as I could remember. It was a dingy, spooky-looking place, straight out of a horror film, with an overgrown garden at the front and shabby curtains at the windows. Curtains that never opened. She never had visitors. In all the time I'd lived in this area, I'd never seen anyone, except for her cat, go in or come out. When I was in junior school, Izzie and I used to think her house was haunted and that Mrs Finkelstein was a witch. Instead of taking the short cut to school through the alley to the right of her house, we used to walk the longer way to avoid passing in case she came out and put a spell on us and we were never seen again. I used to have nightmares about her. She was almost bald and always dressed in a faded black coat and her slippers, and pushed a battered old pram. One day, Izzie and I decided to be brave and made ourselves walk close so that we could see what was in the pram. It was full of old newspapers. Sometimes you'd see her in the shopping area shuffling around, putting discarded papers in the pram. Weird. As I grew older, I realised that she was a harmless eccentric and she didn't scare me so much. Even so, I kept out of her way if I saw her approaching on the same side of the pavement as me.

'So what does her solicitor want?' asked Steve.

'He doesn't say,' said Mum. 'Just that Lal should be at his offices with one of his parents on Friday.'

'Are you sure you haven't done anything, Lal?' said Dad. 'I won't get angry if you tell us, but we need to know what we're dealing with.'

'No, honest,' said Lal. 'I haven't done anything, *honestly*. I know she's a mad old bat, but I never hassle her. In fact, last time I had anything to do with her was on the High Road. Some kids were laughing at her and calling her names and I chased them off. Remember how she always used to shove old newspapers in the pram she pushed around? Well, after I'd seen the kids off, I gave her a few old papers that were lying on a nearby bench. Weird,

I know, but it was the first time I'd ever seen her smile. After that I never had anything to do with her. Honest.'

'Nothing?' asked Mum. 'Think. Think carefully. Something you've forgotten?'

Lal was quiet for a few minutes. 'No. I saw her around, but that was the last exchange we had, if you can call it that. I do talk to her cat though. I always stop to talk to him when I pass her house. He likes to sit on the wall in front and is always up for a tickle under his chin. He's a sweet old boy, blind in one eye with a gammy leg. I feel sorry for him.'

Dad took the letter from Mum, folded it and stuck it behind the clock on the dresser. 'Maybe something's happened to her cat,' said Dad. 'And she's seen you talking to it and, oh I don't know, thought you might have had something to do with it. Who knows what goes on in her mind. Look, don't worry, Lal. Whatever it is she thinks you've done or haven't done, we'll deal with it on Friday. I know what these old timers can be like sometimes. They get an idea into their head about someone and there's nothing you can do to dissuade them. Maybe some other lad has been messing around and upset her. Whatever, we'll put it straight.'

He meant to be reassuring, but Lal looked worried. Clearly I wasn't the only one in our neighbourhood who'd been spooked by Mrs Finkelstein in the past. As I watched him sweat, I wondered if, like me with my mad dream, there was something that he was keeping to himself.

Chapter 5

Candice

News about Candice was all around school by break time on Monday. Candice had told her mate, Jade Wilcocks, who had told Mary O'Connor, who had told Mo Harrison, who told Izzie, who told Nesta and TJ, who told me.

'Apparently she's ten weeks gone already,' said Izzie, as we made our way to the cloakroom.

'Oh God, poor thing,' I said. 'I wonder what she's going to do.'

We didn't have to wait long to find out as she was huddled in the corner of the cloakroom surrounded by her mates. Her eyes were the colour of her hair, red, as she looked like she'd been crying.

Nesta went straight over to her and gave her a hug. 'Hey, Candice. You OK?'

Candice shook her head and looked at the floor. 'I suppose you've heard the news?'

Nesta, TJ, Izzie and I nodded.

'Is there anything we can do?' asked Izzie.

Candice sighed. 'Wave a magic wand and turn back time a few months.'

'What are you going to do?' asked Nesta.

'Nesta!' I said as Candice began to sob. Nesta was never one for subtle questioning.

'I don't know,' she sighed. 'I don't know. What would you do?'

'Well, do your parents know? What do they think?' asked Nesta.

'No,' wailed Candice. 'I haven't told them yet. I mean, what do you say? I got a B in English and oh . . . by the way, I'm having a baby.'

'Yeah. Tough call,' said Nesta, 'but you're going to have to tell them sometime.'

'Not necessarily,' said Mary O'Connor. 'She could always . . . you know . . .'

'Have an abortion, you mean?' asked Nesta.

'That's what I'd do,' said Mo. 'That way no one need ever know about it.'

At this, Candice broke down and started crying properly. 'How can I decide something like that? How can I? I don't know if I could do it. Oh God, my life is *over.* What am I going to do? I *can't* have a baby. I'm only fifteen. I can't believe this is happening. I want to go to college. How am I going to do that with a baby? I won't even be able to get a job.'

'I guess it's a bit late for the Morning-After Pill,' said Izzie.

'Yeah, like ten weeks too late,' groaned Candice. 'You have to take it within seventy-two hours after . . . you know . . .'

'That's what I'd have done,' said Mary. 'I'd have been straight down the birth control clinic and got that pill in time.'

'You could have the baby adopted,' said Jade Wilcocks, 'then you could go to college.'

Candice sniffed. 'But I'd still have to give birth. And it would *hurt*! And everyone would know and say things about me behind my back. Do you think abortion is bad?'

'God, I don't know,' I said. 'I mean, people have them all the time . . . for all sort of reasons.'

'And who can say what's bad or not?' said Izzie. 'I mean, people use all sorts of birth control. If you're going to be really philosophical, you could say that that prevents a baby even having a chance. I don't know. It's a real biggie. I wish God had e-mail sometimes and we could ask him about this sort of thing.'

'My parents are totally against it,' said Mo, 'but I think that it is an option. I mean, if you're not ready to have a baby and you have no support system set up to look after it, why not? Babies cost money and if you're not able to look after it and you don't really want it, then that's not very kind to the baby, is it? So why have it?'

'Does Elliot know?' asked Izzie.

Candice sighed. 'Yes, he knows.'

She looked so sad, drained. I felt really sorry for her. This wasn't the Candice we all knew, always up for a laugh, life and soul of any party.

'But how did it happen?' asked Nesta.

'Duh. We had sex, dummy.'

'Yeah, but didn't you use anything?' Nesta persisted.

Candice nodded. 'Yes. Yes we did. But safe sex isn't always so safe. I think that maybe he didn't put it on in time. I don't know. I don't really know how it happened. We thought we were being so careful. We *were* careful. I bet you all think I'm totally stupid.'

'No way,' said TJ. 'I was a surprise baby. And my parents are both doctors. You'd think if anyone knew all about contraception, it would be them. These things happen.'

'Yeah,' said Izzie. 'It could happen to anyone.'

'Not if you don't have sex,' said Candice. 'Now I wish I hadn't.'

'Was it the first time?' asked TJ.

'No. We'd done it before a couple of times. I don't know what went wrong this time.'

'What does Elliot say?' asked TJ.

Candice leaned over the sink and looked at her face in the mirror. She began to dab her eyes with cold water. 'God, I look a state.' She turned to look at TJ. 'Elliot says it's up to me. It's my decision. He says he'll stand by me whatever I decide, but I don't know if I want to be with him for the rest of my life. But what's the option – be a single mum? I don't know if I could do that either. It's not something you really think about when you're only dating. But what if I do decide to have it and we stay together? How long is he going to hang around? He's only sixteen. If I have the baby, I'll have ruined his life as well. How are we going to pay for it? I don't know. Oh God, I just don't know.' Her eyes started to well up with tears again.

'It might not be so bad,' said Nesta, reaching out and taking Candice's hand. 'Hey, come on. Your parents might be brilliant about it. They might help out and it might turn out to be the best thing that ever happened to you.'

'You don't know my dad,' wailed Candice. 'He'll kill Elliot. He'll kill *me*.'

Nesta squeezed her hand. 'No, he won't. Course he won't. Come on, worst thing he can do is ground you.' She attempted a smile and Candice tried to smile back but couldn't hold it.

Poor, poor Candice, I thought, as I watched her sobbing into the sink. I'd hate to be in her shoes. For me, having babies had only been a dream. For Candice, it was a reality.

Chapter 6

Role Playing

On Thursday night I had a date with Tony. Not a going-out date, I was going over to his parents' flat and we had planned to watch a DVD and chill out. He knew that I was gutted about not being able to go to Italy with the others, so he said he'd get the movie called *A Room With a View*. Some of it is set in Florence and he said he wanted to get it for me so that I wouldn't miss out altogether. I'd been looking forward to it all week but, by the time Thursday came round, I felt sombre. Preoccupied. I kept thinking about Candice crying at school on Monday. What would I do if I were in her shoes? Probably like her, I'd cry a lot. But then what? Being pregnant wasn't something that went away because you didn't want it to be happening. Candice was going to have to deal with it. And make a decision.

It was lovely to see Tony and to snuggle down in his arms to watch the movie. Nesta had gone out to see a musical in the

West End with her parents so we knew we'd be alone for a few hours. All I wanted to do was cuddle up and forget the world, so I hoped he wasn't going to try anything. I wasn't in the mood.

Tony, on the other hand, was in the mood and seemed more interested in snogging than watching the film. When it had finished, he put on Nesta's chill-out compilation and came to sit next to me on the sofa. He put his arm round me and gave me a long smoochy kiss. A few moments later, one of his hands strayed round to my front. I pushed him away. He carried on kissing me, then tried again. Again I pushed him away.

After a few more tries, he pulled away and sat up. 'OK, so what's up, Luce?'

'I'm sorry, Tony, I just not in the right frame of mind . . .' I said.

He faked shock horror. 'Not in the right frame of mind to make out with me? Hhmmm. Must be losing my touch. Here let me try a more subtle approach.'

He threw me back on the sofa, then dived on top of me, nuzzling into my neck and tickling my waist. 'Not in ze mood huh? Ve have vays of getting you in ze mood.'

I laughed and reached back, grabbed a cushion and hit him over the head. 'And ve have vays of fighting back.'

He sat up, raised an eyebrow and grinned wickedly at me. 'Hhhmm. So you vant to fight do you?'

I stood up, armed with my cushion. 'Try me,' I said. I was pretty good with a cushion. I'd had years of training with my two brothers. 'Choose your weapon.'

Tony grabbed a cushion and we went into a great cushion-bashing fight. After a few minutes, he lay back on the sofa and gasped. 'OK, OK. You win. I surrender. I am your slave. I am at your mercy.'

He pulled me on top of him and began to kiss me again. The pillow fight had dispersed the black cloud that had been hovering over me all week and reminded me of why I liked Tony such a lot. He could always make me laugh so, this time, I responded. Once again, after a few moments, he started with the wandering hands. I let him do it for a while and tried to relax, but I couldn't get the image of Candice out of my mind so, after a while, I pushed him off.

'Oh *Lucy*,' he moaned as he sat up. 'What is it with you? Usually you like us being together like this.'

'I know,' I said. 'I'm just not in the mood tonight.'

Tony sighed. 'So when *are* you going to be? There's nothing wrong with it. We've been going together for ages and you know I hold back a lot as it is.'

I sighed. Just what I didn't want to talk about.

Tony sat up for a moment, then looked at me searchingly. 'I need to know what's going on, Luce. You know I want to sleep with you. How long are you going to make me wait?'

I sat in silence for a while, wondering what to say to make it right. 'Don't know,' I said finally.

'Don't know. What's that supposed to mean?'

I felt confused. One part of me wanted to give in to him, another part felt like running away. 'Don't know.'

'Come on, Luce, be reasonable.' He leaned over to me and

snuggled in. 'Give me a break.' Then he sniffed and began to talk in an American accent. 'I'm just a poor lost boy who needs some tender loving care, mam. I've been on the road for many a year now and I'm tired, I'm cold and I'm lonely. What I need is the love of a good woman to restore my faith in mankind.'

We both started to laugh.

'That is a crapola American accent,' I said.

He sat back and grinned up at me. 'Good game though, huh? I saw it on one of those late night sex programmes on TV. They said that in some relationships, it helps to role-play sometimes.'

I rolled my eyes back at him in way of an answer. Tony was always watching stuff like that and reading 'How to be a better lover'-type books. It made me laugh, as he studied them as though he was swotting for a degree in the subject.

He wasn't about to give up. 'Come on, Luce. Let's play that you're a lonely woman out on the prairie and I'm an old experienced cowboy who's been out on the road . . .'

'Who wants to seduce me . . . ?'

'Yeah, you got it!' He smiled.

Nice try, I thought as he sat up and twirled an imaginary moustache.

'How about we play, I'm a very prissy school ma'am,' I said, 'and you're a very naughty boy.'

Tony laughed. 'Yeah. OK. Whatever,' he said. 'As long as I get to seduce you.'

I shook my head and he sighed heavily. I felt mean. It wasn't his fault that I wasn't in the mood for cuddling, never mind having sex. It wasn't him that got Candice pregnant. I decided to try and lighten the atmosphere by making him laugh. I stood up in front of him. 'OK, I've got a role-play for you.' I put one hand on my hip, then bent my other arm and stuck it out at an angle.

He looked bemused. 'Er not sure I get it . . .'

'I'm role-playing. Don't you see? Yoo hoo I'm a teapot.'

Tony cracked up laughing. 'You're bonkers, Lucy Lovering. Hmmm. Yeah. Yoo hoo, I'm a teapot. Yes. Very alluring. Don't think that was one of the examples suggested on the programme, though.'

I sank back on to the sofa and we sat holding hands for a while listening to the music.

After a few moments, Tony turned to me. 'Now, I can't really imagine this for a moment, not unless you're suffering from total brain damage. But . . . are you going off me?'

'No. *No.* Nothing like that,' I reassured him quickly. Even though he'd phrased his question to sound as if he was cool about it, I could tell by his eyes that, behind the bravado, he was feeling insecure and vulnerable. I decided to tell him what was really bothering me. 'This girl at our school has just found out she's pregnant.'

'What's her name?'

'Candice Carter.'

'Wasn't me.'

I punched him. 'I can't stop thinking about her,' I said, 'and what I'd do if it was me. I don't want to end up the same way and, let's be honest, we're definitely heading in that direction.'

Tony sat up and looked at me. 'Just because one girl gets pregnant doesn't mean that you will.'

'I don't want to risk it, Tony.' I snuggled back up to him. 'Why can't we carry on the way we are? Just kissing and cuddling?'

Tony sighed.

'Why not?' I persisted.

He sighed again. 'Because . . . because . . . Oh you know why not.'

'I can't do it, Tony. I'm sorry. I thought I was ready, then . . . well, I'm just not and especially not tonight.'

'Then I don't know if I can carry on like this.'

I sat up. 'Meaning what?'

'Meaning, I don't *want* to carry on like this. It's really difficult. You know I want to take things a stage further and I thought you were into it as well.'

'But . . . oh, Tony, it's not just taking things a stage further. There are risks involved.'

'I've bought condoms,' he said. 'It doesn't have to be a risk.'

'Condoms can split or leak sometimes.'

'I promise I'd be careful.'

Careful, I thought. Just what Candice thought she was being. I shook my head. 'No, sorry Tony, but no. You know I like you more than anyone I've ever met, but I'm not ready. Like, what would you do if I got pregnant?'

'But you won't.'

'You can't guarantee that. What would you do?'

Tony ran his fingers through his hair making it stick up. 'Jeez. I don't know. Don't get heavy about it. We're dating, not starting a family here.'

'But we do have to consider the risks.'

Tony leaned back and chuckled. 'Honest, Luce, I swear that you sound like my mother when you come out with stuff like that.' He began to mimic my voice. 'We have to consider the risks.'

I tried to smile, but it annoyed me that he wasn't taking me seriously. 'I really like you, Tony,' I said. 'You know that don't you?'

'And I like you,' said Tony. 'So why not? It's the most natural thing in the world.'

'Maybe. Yes. Probably. But for one, it's risky and two, it's illegal. You have to be sixteen to have sex legally.'

Tony sat up and took a deep breath. 'I'm eighteen,' he said sadly. 'I'm way legal.'

'I know.'

We sat in silence for a few minutes and the atmosphere felt heavy and uncomfortable. After a while, he reached over and took my hand. 'So what are we going to do?'

'Dunno.'

'How about we take a break for a while, hey?' he asked.

'What do you mean?'

'Well, we've come to the end of the road for us for the time being.'

This wasn't what I wanted to happen. This wasn't what I wanted to hear. 'But why?'

'Because you've just made it very clear that you don't want to go any further with me, so what are we supposed to do? Relationships need to progress and ours isn't doing that. *Can't* do that. We take a step forward, we take a step back. It's not working, Luce, and I'm going out of my mind with frustration.'

I felt numb with disbelief. It was all happening so fast. One minute we're having a pillow fight and cuddling and now . . . he's ending it? It couldn't be happening.

'I don't see why we can't go on as we are,' I said.

He shook his head. 'I don't think I can do that. You and me, well, we've lasted longer than with any other girl I've dated, but I've been holding back for a long time now and I've tried, I've really tried . . .'

'So what are you really saying?'

'Well, actually, you said it first. You're not old enough.'

'I'll be fifteen soon, then sixteen and . . .'

'That's like a year and a bit, Lucy. I can't wait that long. If you're going to make me wait that long, then I'm going to go crazy. We've had a good time, but I feel that if we go on like we have, then we'll start getting at each other. Destroy what we had and that would be a shame because it's been good. I'm sorry, Lucy, but . . .'

'You want to finish?'

He nodded, then sighed. 'It doesn't have to be like this, Luce. I would be really careful. I have done it before.'

'Too much information,' I said, holding up my hand and trying to smile as I said it, but actually I felt like crying. The last thing I wanted to hear about was his other conquests. But then, he was older than me. He had done it before. Maybe it would be OK. Only a few days ago, I'd been seriously considering it, trying to convince myself that there was nobody more perfect to do it with the first time. Then I thought about Candice again. No way, no *way* did I want to be in her shoes.

Tony took my hand and looked at me pleadingly. I felt tears spring to the back of my eyes as I shook my head. We sat in silence again and the atmosphere felt like lead. So much for my great romantic evening, I thought. I couldn't think of anything else to say. There *wasn't* anything else to say. Tony wanted our relationship to progress and it had come to a thundering halt.

'Guess I'd better go, then,' I said.

Tony looked sad, but nodded in agreement. 'I'll walk you home,' he said as he got up.

Nesta called at ten past eleven that night.

'You still awake?' she asked.

'Well, I am now,' I said, sleepily.

'What happened?'

'We broke up.'

'What?! *Why?*'

'I wouldn't go all the way.'

'I'll kill him. Honest, Lucy, I had such a fright. You should have seen me. After what you said the other day about thinking about doing it with Tony, I wondered what you were up to while we were at the theatre. All the lights were off when we got home and no sign of you or Tony. I thought you might be in his room doing the deed. I wanted to give you warning that we were back and ran round switching on lights and the TV, then announcing as loud as I could outside Tony's room that I was going to the bathroom. Mum and Dad thought I was on drugs or something.'

'Had Tony gone to bed?'

'Yeah. I knocked at first in case you were still in there hiding in the wardrobe or something, then, when I realised that you'd gone, I asked where you were. He just muttered, "Gone." When I tried to get more out of him, he told me to go away and shut the door. So, did you really break up?'

'Yeah. We did. The sex thing came up and I decided I wasn't ready.'

'Because of Candice?'

'Sort of. Partly. Plus . . . I don't know, I'd been thinking about it a lot over the last few days. I know not everyone gets pregnant and I know loads of other girls at our school have done it, but I wasn't sure I wanted to be one of them. It all began to feel so complicated and *serious*. I wasn't at all sure what I was feeling and why I was considering going ahead with him. Was it because I was feeling pressured or because I wanted to do it? Plus all the birth control, STD stuff to think about. I don't know, Nesta. No way am I ready for all that.'

'So you're still a virgin?'

'Pure as.'

'Are you OK?'

'Yeah. I will be.'

'I think he's a total creep dumping you because you won't put out.'

'No. It wasn't just that. It really wasn't. He's probably right. He's eighteen. I can't blame him for wanting to take things further. It's more like . . . I don't know, bad timing. He wanted one thing for us, I wanted something else. It wasn't working any more. I'll be OK. It's not like he dumped me because he was bored and had gone off me. To tell you the truth, he looked gutted.'

'I still want to kill him.'

'Look, I want to go to sleep now. See you in school tomorrow.'

'OK. Night.'

Actually, I didn't want to go to sleep. I wanted to think about what had happened. It felt weird. I wasn't sure how I felt. Sad of course, but another part of me felt relieved, like I'd had a close escape. Tony and I had been going with each other on-off for over a year and the sex thing was always at the back of everything, like an unspoken pressure. As Izzie said, a chore on my must-do list. I felt relieved that, for the first time in ages, I had a reprieve. I didn't have to think about any of it for a while – no condoms, no contraception, no planning the right time or place. As I snuggled down in my duvet, I decided I wouldn't be all freaked out about it, like oh, I've been dumped. I've been dumped, poor me. I would move on. I would be positive. Make a new start. All the same, it felt strange. Life without Tony. I was a singleton again.

I got out of bed, got down on my knees and rooted round at the bottom of my wardrobe to find Mr Mackety, my old teddy bear.

'It's you and me again, pal,' I said, as I found him, then got back into bed with him for a cuddle.

Comforts for the Newly Single

Chocolate
Ice cream
Comedy movies
Getting out your old teddy bear
Mates

Chapter 7

Lal and the Lawyer

'I put salt in his coffee this morning,' said Nesta on the way into assembly the next morning. 'You should have seen his face. Served him right.'

'Yeah,' said Izzie. 'And you could sew a few fresh prawns into his duvet and wait for them to go off. He'll be looking everywhere for the smell.'

I laughed, but I didn't think Tony deserved that. I still liked him and he had looked upset at us breaking up. I didn't want him to suffer. 'Give him a break, Nesta. He was being honest, that's all.'

TJ linked her arm through mine. 'Not all boys are like that. You got to move on, Luce. Find a boy who isn't only after one thing.'

'Do they exist?' I asked.

'Yeah. Course,' said Izzie. 'Loads of them.' She didn't look convinced, however.

'Yeah. Boys will be queuing up for you,' said TJ.

I didn't care. I didn't want another boy or another relationship. In fact, I wondered if I'd made a huge mistake last night. Tony must have thought I was such a baby. And pretending to be a teapot? How mad was that? What had I been thinking of? I felt empty. An empty teapot. What if I never found another boy I liked as much? What if I did find a boy and he turned out to be the same as Tony and I was destined to play out the same scene with the wandering hands over and over again? Were all boys only after one thing? And what if Tony started dating soon and I had to hear about it from Nesta? How would it be when I saw him round at her house? As TJ, Nesta and Izzie tried to make me laugh by coming up with more and more outrageous ways of making Tony's life miserable, I found I couldn't join in. I didn't want to talk about him any more.

'From now on, I declare this a Tony-free zone,' I said. 'Let's talk about something else apart from boys, boys, boys.'

Big mistake, I thought, as they all started chatting about their forthcoming trip to Florence. What they were going to take? What outfits? The galleries and museums that they'd be visiting. I couldn't help but feel envious. I so wished I was going with them, but I knew that there was no way. Sometimes life sucks, I thought. They're all going to be off in Italy and I'm going to be home alone with a stuffed toy, watching holiday programmes and wishing I was there.

After school, I raced home as fast as I could as I wanted to make a treat for Lal when he got back. It was the day that he and Mum were going to see Mrs Finkelstein's solicitor and I was worried about what might have happened. I wanted to have something special waiting for him to cheer him up in case it was bad news. I decided to make him his favourite – cheese and tuna melt with a dash of chilli sauce.

I hadn't been back long and had just let the dogs out into the garden when I heard keys in the front door.

'How did it go?' I asked, going out to the hall.

Lal looked at the floor and sighed. 'Bad,' he said. 'Really bad. I have to go to court next week and maybe have to go to prison. The solicitor said I might get five years!'

'What!' I gasped. 'But *why*? What did you do?'

Lal sank on to the stairs and put his head in his hands. 'It's *too* awful.'

Mum slapped Lal lightly over the head. 'You stop that. No, he's not going to prison, Lucy. Nothing like it. He's winding you up. But there is news. Some bad, some good. Is your dad home? And Steve?'

I nodded. 'Dad's out the back in the garage and Steve's in his room. Why? What's happening?'

'Call Steve down, will you, Lucy?' asked Mum as she took her coat off. 'And I'll get your dad. Lal and I have got something to tell you.'

What on earth could it be? I wondered, as I took the stairs two at a time to get Steve.

Five minutes later, we were all gathered around the kitchen table. Even Ben and Jerry had sensed that something was going on and scraped at the back door to come in from the garden. Steve got up to let them in and Ben ran in and came to sit with his head resting on my knees while Jerry took his place next to him, his head resting on Lal's.

'Right,' said Mum. 'Everyone's here. Anyone want a cuppa tea and a bicky before we tell you? I'm famished.'

'*Mum*,' I groaned. 'If you wait another second, I swear I'm going to explode. What's happened?'

Mum looked round at all of us. 'What do you want first? The good or the bad news?'

'Bad news,' said Dad. 'Let's get that over with.'

'OK,' said Mum. 'The bad news is that Mrs Finkelstein died just after Christmas.'

Lal couldn't contain himself any longer. 'And the good news is that she left *me* some money.'

'How much money?' asked Steve.

Lal beamed back at him. 'Rather a lot, actually.'

'Yes. But there is a condition,' said Mum.

After about five minutes, I was wrestling Steve for the phone. Both of us wanted to phone round and tell our mates the good news. He won so I raced upstairs to use my mobile. I couldn't wait to tell Nesta, Izzie and TJ.

'How much?' gasped Izzie.

'Fifty grand. Yeah. I know. Amazing isn't it? It's like winning the lottery.'

'And it's from Mrs Finkelstein? I can hardly believe it.

Remember when we used to think she was a witch?'

'More like a good fairy it turns out. Apparently she was totally loaded. Like mega doshed up. She left most of her money to a cat charity, apart from this one bit to Lal. I'm so happy I could dance.'

'Yeah, but she left it to Lal.'

'I know. But on the way home, he had a chat with Mum and later Dad said it was OK as well. He wants to give every member of our family two grand each as a special pressie. The rest Mum and Dad want him to put in a savings account to see him through college. That's going to be brilliant as well, as Mum and Dad have been trying to put money by ready for when we all go to uni or college or whatever and I don't think they've managed to save much at all.'

'So what are you going to do with yours? Savings account?'

'Some,' I replied, 'but isn't it obvious what I'm going to do with the rest?'

'Hire a killer for Tony?'

'No, dummy. Think.'

'Oh yeah! Course! Florence.'

'Yessss! And I know that those spare places are still going as I heard Miss Watkins telling someone this afternoon.'

'*Brilliant*. Oh Lucy, that will be so top. It wouldn't have been the same going without you. Now our whole gang will be there.'

'I'm going to phone TJ now and tell her. Will you phone Nesta for me? I don't want to risk Tony answering. I'm not ready to play out that scene yet.'

'Yeah, course.'

Next I called TJ. Like Izzie, she was over the moon when I told her the news and realised that I could go to Italy with them.

'So what's the condition on Lal getting the money?'

'He has to look after Mrs Finkelstein's cat. It's so funny as we were all worried that Lal'd done something to upset her when, all along, she'd put him in her will. Dunno how Ben and Jerry are going to feel about having an old cat around but, hey, no one's going to say no to fifty grand are they? We'll get them some luxury dog food or something to soften the blow.'

'But why did she leave it to Lal?'

'He used to talk to her cat on his way home from school sometimes. She must have seen him and clocked it. Lal's a real softie on the quiet you know, especially where animals are concerned. He buys dog food with his pocket money sometimes and leaves it out for the fox. Since we got wheelie bins in our neighbourhood, Lal has been worried that foxie couldn't get leftovers from the rubbish any more. But Florence, I'm coming to Florence. It's amazing, isn't it?'

'Totally,' said TJ. 'Just shows that you never know what's round the next corner.'

'But we do this time. Florence!'

Life *is* full of surprises, I thought after she'd hung up. Only this morning, I'd thought there was no way, no how I could go on the school trip and now, not even twenty-four hours later, everything's changed. Not only can I go, but I'll have some spending money as well. Perfect, perfect way to get over Tony. *Viva*, I'm off to sunny . . . um, . . . Italy, *viva* um, *Italia*.

Revenge Ideas

Sewing fresh prawns into his duvet. *Nesta*
Sewing up the ankles of his trousers. *TJ*
Tie his shoelaces together. *Lucy*
I don't think revenge is good for the soul. Forgiveness is better. But then, if I was pushed for a suggestion, I reckon you can't beat getting hold of his mobile phone, then phoning the automatic time in Hong Kong. *Izzie*

Chapter 8

Take-off

'Passport?' asked Nesta.

'Check,' chorused Izzie, TJ and I.

'Lip-gloss.'

'Check,' we chorused again.

'Condoms.'

I hit Nesta over the head. 'No, definitely not. No condoms. I don't want to see them, hear about them or think about them for some considerable time. Or boys for that matter. Time off. I'm having a holiday from all that stuff.'

Nesta pulled a face. 'Yeah sure, until you meet some cutenik on the plane . . .'

'Nope. I'm serious. Not interested.'

I looked out of the coach window at the dark February morning. I didn't care that it was wet and gloomy or an unearthly time to be up on a Saturday. I didn't care that we were stuck in traffic. We were on the M4 heading for Heathrow airport. On our way. I felt so excited. I'd hardly slept a wink last night thinking about it. Italy. It was actually happening. A whole week in Florence with my mates. OK, so our teachers, Mrs Elwes and Mr Johnson, and twenty-one other pupils were with us, but that didn't matter. A week without school, sharing a room with TJ, Izzie and Nesta. Bliss. I'd never been to Europe before. I'd never even been on a plane before, as our family usually took holidays in England in Devon or on the south coast somewhere. This was to be my first time abroad. As we turned off the motorway on to the exit for the airport, I heard a roar to my left: a plane was taking off, up, up and over the cars on the motorway and into the sky.

And then it hit me. In about two hours, I would be on one of those great metal contraptions. Strapped into a seat. My first time. I made myself breathe. I can't do it, I thought as I felt myself go hot, then cold. I can't. It's not natural. I mean, how does a thing that size and that weight even get off the ground? Suddenly the floodgates in my head opened and every bad news story about planes from the past five years decided to replay in my head. Oh not now, not now *please*, I told myself. No. I'm cool. I *must* be cool. The others will think I'm a big scaredypants if I suddenly announce that I'm frightened of flying.

'You OK, Luce?' asked TJ. 'You've gone kind of quiet.'

'Um, yeah. Just thinking . . .'

'Aren't you excited?'

'Yeah. Yeah. Course, I will be when we get there, but . . . but

I've never flown before and . . .'

'Piece of cake,' said Nesta. 'No worries. Lovely, up in the air and the clouds beneath you. Fab.'

'How high up exactly?' I asked.

'About thirty-five thousand feet.'

I felt myself shiver. Oh dear, that's high, I thought. And once you're in and up, no chance of getting out. It's not like the Tube or the bus where you can get off at the next stop if you feel wobbly.

TJ reached over and put her hand on mine. 'Don't worry,' she said. 'I used to be scared of flying, but statistics show that it's safer than crossing the road. I read that somewhere. The journey's only a few hours. We'll be there before you know it.'

I attempted a weak smile back. 'Hope so,' I said.

The airport was heaving with people of every age, shape and nationality. Some irate and in a hurry, some looking apprehensive like me, others stretched wearily over chairs checking the monitor about delayed flights, others aimlessly wandering about clutching their hand luggage and waiting for their flight call. People eating, drinking, shopping, changing money, spending. I'm glad I'm travelling with a group, I thought, as Mrs Elwes led us to the check-in desk. The number of people travelling was overwhelming. I think I'd have found it all too much on my own.

At the check-in, an old couple were causing a commotion, as they didn't seem to know what they were doing or where they should be.

'What airline are you flying with?' asked the flight attendant behind the desk.

'Pardon?' the old lady shouted. 'You'll have to speak up, I'm a bit deaf.'

'Airline?' repeated the flight attendant. The old lady looked confused so the flight attendant raised her voice. 'WHO ARE YOU FLYING WITH?'

At this the old lady smiled and pointed to an even more ancient looking man with her. 'UNCLE BERNARD,' she shouted back.

I got the giggles and Mrs Elwes turned round and frowned at me. Luckily, the old couple finally realised what the flight attendant was really asking and soon our group was checked in, our luggage labelled and sailing away on a conveyer belt.

After that, it was through Passport Control and security where Mr Johnson was stopped and searched. At the sight of the young female security officer feeling up and down our bald and bespectacled teacher's trouser legs, our whole group started giggling.

'Probably the most fun he's had in years,' whispered Nesta.

'I hope you girls are going to behave on this trip,' said Mrs Elwes, trying to shush us up by waving her hands, but I could see that she was having a hard time not cracking up as well.

We nodded back at her. 'Best behaviour, promise,' said Nesta.

'Right then,' she said, once the last of us was through and had collected our hand luggage. 'We have some time before departure, so you can have a wander if you like. You can either meet Mr Johnson or myself here in half an hour precisely or listen out for any announcements saying that our flight is ready for boarding and make your own way. If for any reason anyone gets lost, check the monitors and make your way to the departure gate posted. In *plenty* of time. You're Year Ten so I expect you to act like responsible adults. Never forget that we're travelling as a school and we represent that school. Understood?'

The twenty-five of us nodded, then took off in various directions to explore the shops. We knew what to do when the time came to board. Mrs Elwes had been over it all enough times in class, plus she'd handed out leaflets on the coach about procedure.

The departure area was brightly lit with shops and cafés and took my mind off flying for a while. We tried on perfumes in Duty Free, dabbled with make-up samples, bought mags in WH Smith, explored the bookshops, tried on jewellery in Accessorize, mooched about in the clothes shops, had Cokes and before we knew it an hour had passed.

'Oh Lord,' said Nesta, as she checked her watch, then glanced up at the monitor.

'Oh poo,' said Izzie. 'Our flight started boarding ten minutes ago.'

'Will the following passengers please go to Gate Number 12,' came an announcement over the intercom, 'where their flight to Florence is ready to depart. Isobel Foster, Theresa Watts, Nesta Williams and Lucy Lovering.'

'Ohmigod, that's us,' said TJ. 'Oh crapola and a half.'

She began to run to a passage where there was a sign saying

which gates were where and we raced after her at top speed. The sign also said that some gates were five minutes away, some ten minutes and some twenty. Of course, Gate 12 was one of the last.

'I don't think we're going to make it,' panted TJ, as we pelted along the tunnel almost knocking over passengers coming the other way.

'We have to,' said Nesta. 'We can't get this far . . .'

'Mrs Elwes is going to kill us,' said TJ.

'What's she going to do?' I asked as I ran along side her. 'Tell us we're grounded when we're thirty-five thousand feet up in the air.'

Izzie started laughing and had to stop and hold her sides. '*Don't* make me laugh when I'm running a marathon.'

After a breathtaking sprint down long corridors, in the distance, I spotted a familiar tall blonde woman.

'I can see Mrs Elwes,' I called over my shoulder and at last we were there. We hurtled into the small seating area by the Gate as the last passengers were making their way into the tunnel leading to the plane. Mr Johnson was pacing up and down by the desk and looking at his watch.

'Sorry, sir,' said Nesta, as she raced up to him and used the excuse guaranteed to work with most male teachers. 'Er . . . girls' thing, period problem . . . Had to get last minute supplies . . . I can explain . . .'

Mr Johnson immediately looked at the floor and waved us ahead of him. 'Right. Right. No need to explain. Um. Carry on.'

'Yes, sir, sorry,' said Izzie as she overtook him.

'You girls will be the death of me,' he said, shaking his head and mumbling as he followed us on to the plane. 'I don't know why I got talked into this trip. Madness. I should be going to Scotland for a bit of quiet fishing. On my own. Yes, madness, madness to have agreed.'

Once on the plane, he settled down and put his newspaper over his head and Nesta found our seats on the left-hand side of the cabin at the back.

'He's just stopped smoking,' said Mo Harrison as she shoved her coat into the overhead compartment. 'Best keep out of his way for a few days.'

'Do you want to sit in the window seat or aisle?' asked TJ pointing at the seats in front of Nesta and Izzie. 'You choose as it's your first flight.'

'Oh, sit at the window,' said Nesta, 'then you can look out.'

I did as she said, but I wasn't sure about it. Once on board, my panic had returned. The inside of the aeroplane looked too small to have so many people tightly packed in. It felt airless and I felt suffocated. I just wanted to get the whole thing over with.

As soon as everyone was seated, the plane began to taxi along the runway and a female voice on an intercom welcomed us aboard.

'OK, Luce?' asked TJ.

I nodded and gripped the sides of my seat.

'Eyes right,' Nesta whispered from behind us. 'Looks like we're not the only school doing a trip to Florence.'

I glanced over to my right and sure enough there was another group. Boys. About twenty of them and, as we were eyeing them, they were eyeing us back. They looked well pleased to have spotted a group from an all girls' school on their journey.

'Let the holiday commence,' said Nesta.

'In case of emergency . . .' continued the female voice over the intercom as the flight attendants went into the safety procedure at the top of each aisle.

One dark-haired boy with a cheeky face, who was sitting opposite us, introduced himself as Liam and took it upon himself to give a running commentary along with the voice-over. He leaned over to us. 'What she's saying in short is, we crash, you die.'

'Oh thanks a lot,' I said, but TJ laughed.

Later when the flight attendant gave instructions as to what to do if we went down over water, Liam leaned over again.

'The light is to attract any sailors, as in "Hello, sailor" and the whistle is to attract the attention of any passing sharks.'

TJ laughed again and they got chatting. I, in the meantime, was having a religious moment and had decided to appeal to higher powers. Dear God or whoever's up there and whatever you like to be called, I prayed, please let this plane go up and down without any problems. I know I probably could have been a better person and prayed more often, but I promise that if only you let this plane take off, and land, and fly, I will be positively saintly and do no end of good deeds.

An enormous thrust and roar from the engines and we were taking off. I gripped my seat tighter. I glanced out of the window. Big mistake as landmarks beneath us began to look smaller and smaller, and in minutes it was like looking out over a toy town as the houses and cars became dots as we took off into the sky. Suddenly we hit cloud and I couldn't see anything.

'Ohmigod, we're going to crash,' I gasped, clutching TJ's arm. 'The pilot won't be able to see. What if there's another plane in the sky? He won't be able to see it.'

'They fly by their instruments,' said TJ. 'Don't worry. All other traffic will show up on his monitors.'

'I don't like it,' I said and shut my eyes tight, then opened them again.

Unluckily, Liam noticed and, as soon as the announcement came on saying that we could undo our seat belts, he came over with his mate and leaned over our seats.

'Your mate chicken, then?' Liam asked TJ.

'Chicken!' chortled Nesta behind us. 'I'd stay away from her if I were you, sonny. Don't let her hear you saying things like that. It can get her mad and that's not a pretty sight. She may be small, but she's lethal. Think *Charlie's Angels*. Think *Kill Bill* . . .'

Think *Winnie-the-Pooh*, I thought, but I didn't like to interrupt her when she was on a roll.

'In fact,' she continued, 'we're on our way to an anger management convention to see if they can help her. We had to sedate her for the flight in case she took a dislike to anyone on board. So take my advice and push off.'

As soon as Liam's mate clocked Nesta, his eyes lit up. 'Now this flight is getting interesting,' he said and moved down the aisle to chat to her.

'Some boys just can't take a hint, can they?' asked TJ, glancing over her shoulder.

Izzie leaned forward from behind us and handed me a small bottle. 'Here's some Bach Flower Remedy,' she said. 'Put a few drops under your tongue.'

'Thanks,' I said.

'What's it for?' asked TJ.

'Anxiety,' whispered Izzie. 'It helps people chill. It's totally natural. It's from Lucy's dad's shop.'

I took the bottle and dropped a little on to my tongue. I'd seen it on the shelves at the shop but never tried it before. It tasted of alcohol.

'See,' said Nesta in a loud voice. 'I *told* you we had to sedate her. Something's upset her and we're having to up her medication.'

I felt myself turning bright red as all the boys in the middle aisle turned and stared at me with my bottle of Bach Flower Remedy.

Suddenly the plane took another lurch upwards and my stomach went with it.

'It's going to be OK,' said TJ as I clutched her arm again. 'Listen. You have to trust that the pilot knows what he's doing. He's trained. Millions of planes take off every day all over the world without incident . . .'

I put my fingers in my ears. 'Don't like it . . .'

'Those noises are good. It means that the plane is doing what it's meant to do,' said TJ. 'If you understood the mechanics of it, you wouldn't be scared at all. It's only because you don't that you're frightened but, honestly, there's nothing to worry about.'

'Have some more Bach Flower Remedy,' said Izzie. 'And if that doesn't work I've got some lavender essential oil that you can dab on your forehead to relax you.'

'Nah. Forget that New-Age mumbo jumbo,' said Nesta. 'Check out the boys. Nothing like a cute boy to distract the mind.'

I decided to do as Nesta instructed and glanced over at the boys to do a quick scan. Nope, not one I fancy, I thought. Not one of them was a patch on Tony, but then he was exceptionally good-looking. I felt sad that things had ended the way they had. He had tried to phone me last night, when Nesta, TJ and I slept over at Izzie's ready for the early flight this morning. Nesta had told him to pick on someone his own age as she was still mad at him on my behalf, but I couldn't help but wonder what it was he wanted. Probably just to say goodbye as he's nice like that and we've always been good friends, I thought.

After half an hour or so, we were served a breakfast of a stale croissant and a cup of bitter-tasting coffee. Instead of eating, the boys seemed to think it was funny to start a food fight and began chucking their croissants around until they got a telling off from one of their teachers. They soon chilled out as the teacher looked scary – a bit like Professor Snape in *Harry Potter*.

He didn't put our girls off, however, and as the flight went on, most of our group got chatting to the lads. Nesta moved over into the middle aisle and was soon surrounded by admirers, all fighting for her attention as usual. A handsome Indian boy took Nesta's place and seated himself next to Izzie. TJ moved off to talk to Liam and I could hear her laughing down the aisle. At one point, a dark-haired boy looked over at me and raised an eyebrow as if to say how about it? He was handsome in an overblown way that doesn't appeal to me. Big mouth, big eyebrows. He looked well sure of himself.

'Hi. I'm Chris,' he said, then winked at me.

I made my eyes go cross-eyed. That put him off. He wasn't my type. Not one of them was my type. It would be a long time before I saw some one who could compare to Tony.

'Practise,' mouthed Nesta from the centre of the plane.

I shook my head. I wasn't even in the mood for practice flirting. What was the point? I refastened my seat belt, put my head in my magazine, then let myself drift off thinking about Tony. I let myself imagine what it might have been like going away with him, how he'd hold my hand when the plane took off, how he'd put his arm round me to reassure me when the engines got noisy . . .

'Lucy, Lucy, we're here,' said TJ's voice in my ear. 'Wake up.'

I sat up and rubbed my eyes. 'What? Where? Where am I?'

'Italy!' announced Nesta.

I glanced out of the window to see airport buildings and the runway. 'What we've landed and everything?'

'Yep, and you snored and dribbled all the way through it,' said TJ. 'The whole plane was laughing.'

'Did not.' I punched her.

'You were well gone. I tried to wake you, but you just took my hand, put your head on my shoulder and called me Tony.'

'Sorry,' I said. 'It must have been because I didn't sleep much last night, then we had to get up at the crack of dawn.' I was glad I'd slept through the landing. It was the part I'd been dreading most. But now it was over, we'd landed and were well and truly in Italy.

It didn't take long to get through Customs and pick up our luggage, and soon we were outside the airport where the girls were full of gossip about the boys and who'd said what to whom.

'Guess I missed a lot when I nodded off,' I said, as Mrs Elwes marched us towards the exit.

'Nah, not really,' said Nesta. 'Anyway the boys are staying at the same hotel as us so you can soon catch up.'

'Oh no,' I groaned. 'So am I going to be Billy Loner for the trip while you all get off with the boys on the plane?'

'No way,' said Nesta. 'There was no one there I liked, but it looks as though TJ and Izzie have scored.'

TJ grinned. 'No one serious,' she said. 'Not on holiday. The guy I was talking to was a laugh, but he's a bit of a show off and the group he's with seem a right load of plonkers.'

'Boys in a group,' said Nesta. 'They always act tougher than they are.'

'And more stupid,' said Izzie. 'But the boy who sat next to me, Jay, he was nice.'

'Oh God,' said Nesta, as we got outside the airport building and Mrs Elwes stopped at a battered-looking bus and started talking to the driver. 'I thought Florence was the city of style.'

'It is,' I said, as I noticed an elegant black limousine that had just drawn up behind the bus. 'I see my private transport has arrived. Excuse me, girls. I'll see you back at the hotel, that is if your old jalopy makes it.' I flounced off towards the limo doing my best cat walk strut.

Nesta coughed loudly. I turned back to look at her and she pointed at a pillar to my left, behind which was a tall boy with floppy blond hair who was watching me with an amused look on his face.

He stepped forward. He was cute, dressed in jeans, a black parka and baseball cap. It was hard to judge how old he was, maybe sixteen, maybe seventeen.

'Your car awaits, ma'am,' he said in an American accent, then doffed his cap. 'Can I give you a ride?'

'Why sure you can, young man,' I replied in my best American accent.

As he opened the back door for me, the chauffeur turned from the driver's seat and gave him a quizzical look.

I looked around for the owner of the car. I didn't want to get into trouble before we'd even left the airport. 'Hey, whoever owns this car might not like us messing about with it,' I said, 'and the chauffeur doesn't look too pleased.'

The boy grinned. 'Oh he's cool. The car's for me. My dad sent it for me. Allow me to introduce myself. Teddy Ambrosini Junior.'

Oh Lord, he really is an American, I thought as I went scarlet. 'Lucy Lovering. Junior. Um. Sorry. Didn't realise.'

'Why would you? So can I give you a lift some place?'

'Um. No. Only joking. Here with . . . friends.' I indicated our group with a sweep of my hand.

He glanced over at the group from our school, who were all standing staring. Izzie, Nesta and TJ were laughing their heads off.

'You got a lot of friends,' he said.

'Yes. I um, like people. Lots of them.'

'Cool. Me too. So. Your first visit to Florence?'

I nodded. 'Sightseeing. Can't wait. You?'

'Funeral.'

Oh God. I felt myself blushing. 'Oh. Sorry. I just assumed . . . Um . . .'

'It's OK. You weren't to know.'

'Someone you knew?' I asked, then I wanted to slap myself. What a dumb question. Why on earth would he be attending a funeral of someone he didn't know?

'My grandmother.'

I felt really awkward. 'Oh. A relative, then?' Oh God. More stupid. Stupid me. Course she's a relative. 'I mean . . .'

Teddy smiled. 'Yeah. She was a relative. My father's family live over here. My gran was here in Florence. My dad's based in Milan though. I come over a few times a year since my folks broke up. Where are you staying?'

'Hotel Renoldo or Revoldo or Revanoldo. Somewhere. In Florence. You?'

'Hotel Villa Corelli.'

'Lucy Lovering,' called Mr Johnson, 'on the bus now.'

The boy grinned. 'Looks like one of your friends wants you.'

I grinned sheepishly. 'Teacher. School trip.'

'Thought so,' he said. 'Well have a good trip, Lucy Lovering Junior. Maybe see you around.'

'Yeah,' I said. 'Maybe.'

What a great name and what amazingly white teeth, I thought as I got on the bus with the others. And what a fab voice. Low and sultry. Shame I totally blew it by acting like the dumbest person to arrive from Dumbland.

Flight Tips

Bach Flower Rescue Remedy to steady nerves.

Lavender oil for calming. (A few drops on a tissue then inhale, or rub a few drops into the temple.)

Eucalyptus oil (a few drops on a tissue then inhale. Eucalyptus is a natural antiviral and can kill any germs circulating in the cabin and help prevent getting other people's holiday viruses.)

Take earplugs and an eye mask if you want to sleep.

Chapter 9

Firenze

'Keetchen closed,' growled an acne-pocked man behind the reception desk at our hotel.

'We only wanted a sandwich or something,' insisted Mrs Elwes. 'A snack? These girls have been travelling since early this morning.'

'Keetchen closed,' he repeated and turned away.

Mrs Elwes turned to us and rolled her eyes. 'OK. Line up girls and get your room keys from Mr Johnson. I suggest we go and dump our bags. Have a quick wash, then meet back here and we'll go straight into the centre for a bite to eat.'

'Fantabuluso,' said TJ as Mr Johnson handed her a key.

'Now we'll get to see the real Florence,' said Nesta. '*Firenze*. That's Florence in Italian!'

I hoped we would, as my first impressions of Italy from the bus had been disappointing. Motorway, building sites, traffic, and the hotel looked like any other hotel in the world on the outside – a five-storey building in a busy suburb. The weather was grey like back in the UK and it was nothing like the Florence I'd seen in the film *A Room With a View*.

I followed the girls up to the first floor, which is where our room was, and wondered what Teddy's hotel was like. If it was anything like the limo, it would be spectacular.

'Oh,' said Izzie, as TJ unlocked our door and we stepped inside a room the size of a broom cupboard. There were two bunk beds crammed in on either side, a tiny wardrobe, an ancient-looking TV on top of a rickety cabinet and a set of drawers. The only nice thing in the room was an antique lamp with red beading around the shade.

'Bagsy the top,' I said as I slung my rucksack on the top bunk on the left of the room.

'OK,' said Nesta as she headed straight for the cupboard under the TV set. 'At least it's got a minibar.'

Two minutes later, she was handing round pieces of chocolate she'd found in the minibar. I munched on my bit, then got up on to my bunk and lay back to enjoy our new surroundings.

'Ah, luxury,' I said as I gazed up at the ceiling. The paint was peeling off in places and the shadow in the right corner looked distinctly like damp.

TJ slid open a door to the side of the room and stuck her head in. 'Well, at least we've got a shower and loo. That's something.'

'As long as we're not expected to sleep in it,' I said. 'Although it might be more comfy than this. These pillows are really lumpy.'

'Never mind,' said Nesta through a mouthful of chocolate. 'We won't be spending much time in here.'

Izzie peered through a small window behind the TV. 'Oh the beauty of Italy,' she sighed.

I got down to go and look. I laughed when I saw that all that was visible from the window was a brick wall opposite. 'So much for a room with a view.'

A moment later there was a knock at our door.

'Reception in five minutes, girls,' Mrs Elwes called through.

'But we haven't unpacked,' said Izzie.

'We won't need much,' said Nesta as she threw her hand luggage into the minuscule wardrobe. 'I've got a few Euros that Dad gave me – enough to last us this afternoon, then we can change the rest of our money later.'

'Shall we take mobiles?' I asked. I was really chuffed because Nesta's dad had had all our mobiles upgraded so that we could use them abroad. I was dying to phone someone on mine, even if it was just Izzie in the next bed.

Izzie pulled a face. 'Mine's at the bottom of my bag. Let's leave them. We'll all be together so we won't need them.'

I pulled a few things out of my rucksack and threw them in the wardrobe with my hand luggage.

'Why have you brought that load of stuff?' asked Nesta as she spotted my sewing basket on top of my clothes. 'We're supposed to be on holiday.'

'A true artist never travels without the tools of her trade,' I replied. 'You never know when inspiration will strike. I might see some fab fabric and, according to the schedule Mrs Elwes gave us, we haven't got much on in the evenings.'

'You're here to *relax,'* said Nesta as she locked our money up in the small safe that she found in one of the drawers. 'Give yourself a break and buy some ready-made stuff. I've heard that the markets are full of fab stuff.'

Ten minutes later, we were back on the bus and on our way into the centre. As the bus made its way over the River Arno, down busy streets lined with shops, Florence started to look more interesting. I felt my eyes popping out of my head as I took in the brightly-lit windows displaying gorgeous-looking clothes and designs, and I couldn't wait to start exploring. The bus stopped on a street in the centre and we got off and headed straight for the nearest pizzeria. After a Coke and a slice of pizza, Mrs Elwes and Mr Johnson announced that it was time to start the tourist trail.

'First stop, the station,' she said and marched us off down a busy street.

'She's been before,' said Mr Johnson, who took up the rear of our group. 'Knows her way round.'

I'm glad one of us does, I thought as we followed her down a busy street.

As I battled to keep upright in the jostling crowds, I couldn't help but feel that there must be more to the place. I'd seen great shops, great window displays, loads of cafés, but I wondered what the fuss about Florence being a magical romantic place was all about. It looked like any big, bustling city to me.

At a kiosk, Mrs Elwes bought tickets for an open-topped sightseeing bus and we all piled on and upstairs.

'Fantastic,' said Nesta, as the bus chugged off and we sat back to take in the sights.

'Easily the best way to see the city on the first trip, even though it is a tad chilly,' said Mrs Elwes, who took a seat in front of us and wrapped her coat tightly round herself. 'When I first came with my husband, we wore ourselves out walking all over the place. This way, you can see it all, get your bearings and you cover more ground than you ever could on foot.'

'Nice one, Mrs Elwes,' said Izzie, who was never one for long walks.

The bus tour was definitely the way to do it, especially for a shortie like me. On the street, I felt like I was going to be crushed at any minute but, up on the bus, I could see clearly. Every street seemed to have something worth looking at. We'd turn a corner and there would be a glorious building, a group of amazing statues or work of sculpture. This is more how I imagined it, I thought, as I sat back to take it all in.

'That's the Duomo,' said Mrs Elwes, as we passed an enormous golden cathedral with beautiful carvings on the doors. 'It dates back to 1294. And that marble building in the square opposite, that's the Baptistry. Look to your right as we go past at the stunning door. It's called the Gate to Paradise.'

'Oh, wow!' said Nesta. She pointed down towards the Duomo. 'Definitely a place to investigate.'

I looked to where she pointed, and saw that she wasn't looking at the magnificent doors or the architecture, but rather at the steps where there were hoards of teenagers hanging out.

'Over there, over there,' said Nesta waving madly at a bunch of cute-looking boys who looked up and waved back.

'Ding *dong*,' said Izzie and gave her the thumbs up. 'Magnificent examples of early twenty-first century sculpture, I do believe. Why, they almost look alive!'

Mrs Elwes looked at Izzie and smiled approvingly. 'I'm so pleased that you appreciate art,' she said.

'Er . . . um, yes,' said Izzie. 'Art.'

'Imagine how it must have been before the traffic and the tourists,' said TJ. 'It must have been fab.'

Nesta pulled a face. The tourists, of the male variety, were clearly what she found most interesting.

After a while the bus passed back over the River Arno where Mrs Elwes pointed out a bridge with houses on it in the distance. 'Ponte Vecchio,' she said. 'That's where all the jewellery shops are.'

'Lead the way,' said Nesta, smiling. 'Sounds like my kind of sightseeing.'

The bus wound its way up a hill, past stunning old villas in shady grounds and up to a square that Mrs Elwes told us was called Piazza Michelangelo. The hilltop view was panoramic. Stretched out in front of us was the river, the Old Town, the Duomo, towers and churches, red-roofed buildings. It looked wonderful. The light was just starting to fade and the whole city was bathed in a rosy glow. Now this is more like a scene from the movie, I thought as I gazed around me. It's just a question of finding the right places. Like in any city, there are the old interesting bits and the new bland bits, like the area we drove through on the way to the hotel from the airport.

'From here, it looks like a place from a different era,' I said.

'It is,' said TJ. 'The Renaissance.'

'Old you mean,' said Izzie, but she looked well impressed.

'Anyone seen the movie, *A Room With a View*?' asked Mrs Elwes.

I nodded.

'Remember the scene where the Helena Bonham Carter character, what was her name in the film? Can't remember! Anyway, she opens her window in the beginning and we see Florence for the first time?'

I nodded again.

'Well that was filmed from somewhere around here,' said Mrs Elwes, pointing to the left of the square. 'From just down there, I think.'

'I *thought* so,' I said.

On a plinth in the middle of the square, gazing out over Florence, towered a giant statue of naked man. It looked as though whoever made it set out to create a perfect face and body.

'He looks like he worked out,' said Nesta as she took in the fabulous muscles on his legs and arms.

'That's Michelangelo's *David*, but not the original,' Mrs Elwes told us. 'There are two copies of it, in fact. One here and one in one of the squares in the centre. The original is in the Galleria dell'Accademia.

Nesta looked the statue up and down. 'Nice butt,' she said and took a photo.

Mrs Elwes rolled her eyes. 'You're looking at one of the greatest works of art in the world and all you can comment is "nice bum".'

'Well it is.' Nesta shrugged.

Mrs Elwes looked again. 'Yes,' she said, grinning. 'I suppose it is.'

'This is my favourite bit of Florence so far,' I said as I looked around. 'It's how I imagined it would be.'

'What looking at David's bottom?' asked Nesta.

'No stupid, the view, the sense of history. You can really feel it up here.'

'Ah, but there's so much more,' said Mrs Elwes with a smile.

I took a deep breath. So much more, I thought. I hoped so. I'm almost fifteen and I've hardly seen anything of the world and yet there is so much to see. Cities like this in Europe, America, the Far East. Places filled with people all living their lives in locations so different to my familiar one in North London.

As the bus continued its tour, it took us back down the hill past more stately old houses and villas in their own grounds. I pointed to one that looked like a grand country house with shuttered windows and beautiful terraced grounds with statues and fountains and trees.

'That place looks the business,' I said as we passed by.

'Villa Corelli it says on the sign,' said Izzie. 'Someone very posh must live there.'

'Villa Corelli?' I asked. 'I think that's where Teddy said he was staying. Is it a hotel?'

'Grand Hotel Villa Corelli. One of Florence's finest,' said Mrs Elwes. 'I went there for cocktails once. That was all we could afford. I can't imagine what it costs to stay there.'

I looked to see if I could see Teddy anywhere in the grounds, but there didn't seem to be anybody about. 'Maybe we could sneak in for a Coke one day,' I suggested.

'A Coke?' asked Nesta. 'Somehow I don't think it's just a Coke that you want there.'

I punched her. 'I told you. I am not interested in boys on this trip and, anyway, we'll probably never see Teddy again.'

'Teddy,' Nesta said with a laugh. 'What kind of name is that?'

'I like it,' I said. 'It's a cuddly name.'

Nesta raised an eyebrow at me.

'Stop it,' I said. 'His name is cuddly. It doesn't mean I want to cuddle him.'

'Yeah right,' said Nesta and gave me one of her knowing looks.

The bus drove back over the river, into the centre and let us off outside an ice cream shop.

'Now this is what I really call art,' said Izzie as she took in what was on offer. There was every flavour imaginable described in English and Italian – pineapple, banana, strawberry cheesecake, raspberry, kiwi, pistachio, vanilla, coffee, chocolate to name only a few.

'Fab, fab, fab,' I said as TJ handed me a double pecan fudge and I took a lick. 'Art. Culture. History. Statues with great bums. Fashion. Great ice cream. This place is growing on me.'

'It will if we keep eating these ice cream gelato thingees,' said Izzie. 'Literally, it will grow on your bum. But . . . well, I can't resist. Yum.'

'And now to my favourite place,' said Mrs Elwes. 'Just a quick look before we go back to our hotel as we've had a long day.'

Mr Johnson didn't have an ice cream and I saw him looking longingly at a man at a bus stop who was smoking a cigarette. Why want one of those, I thought, when you can have ice cream instead? They smell disgusting and make you ill and make you miserable if you can't have one. I hoped I'd never get addicted.

Mrs Elwes led us down a street, then turned a corner and we found ourselves in a large square lined with open air cafés. To the far right, there was a collection of statues. They looked unlike so many of the statues back in England, where the subject was still. These looked animated – arms reaching towards the sky and limbs bent as if ready to take off at any minute.

'This is Piazza Della Signoria,' said Mrs Elwes. 'It's where the Uffizi museum is and is my favourite of all the squares. The Uffizi is over on the right near the statues. We'll visit there tomorrow. Now, Mr Johnson and I are going to get a drink in the café over there and you girls can either join us or have a wander. Don't go out of the square as there's enough to see here for now. Meet back here at six on the dot. Have those of you who have upgraded mobiles got them?'

'Oh no, I left mine at the hotel,' I whispered. 'It's in my hand luggage.'

'So did I,' chorused TJ and Izzie.

'And me,' said Nesta. 'They barely gave us a minute to get organised. Just nod and smile. We'll be fine. We won't need them.'

As Mrs Elwes and Mr Johnson headed off for the café, Izzie, Nesta, TJ and I made for the statues. On the way we passed a gold statue of an Egyptian mummy.

'Strange that this is here,' said TJ going up close to get a better look. 'All the other statues are white and look Roman.'

The statue turned and winked at her.

'Woah,' she cried and leaped back in shock.

'A mime,' I said.

'Brilliant,' she said as she recovered. 'I don't know how they keep so still.'

'Must be very boring,' said Izzie, 'standing like that all day.'

The statue gave her a deep bow, then clapped. Whoever was behind the costume must have understood English.

After the mummy, we went to look at the statues. Like *David* in the Piazza Michelangelo, they were all enormous and naked. It was awesome to gaze up at the great, sculpted bodies towering into the sky.

'*Perseus* by Benvenuto Cellini,' said TJ, who had brought along a guide book. '*Rape of a Sabine* by Giambologna, *Hercules and Cacus* by Bandinelli . . .'

I couldn't resist it. 'Um . . . I wonder if she was,' I said.

'Was what?' asked TJ.

'Bandy. You know, Nelly. I wonder if she was bandy. Bandy Nelly. Not a very kind nickname.'

TJ patted my head. 'Just keep taking the tablets, Lucy,' she said, then went back to her guidebook. '*Judith and Holofernes* by Donatello.'

'I wonder if Bandy Nelly had a sister. Knock-kneed Nellie,' I said and I began to walk about as if I were knock-kneed.

Nesta and Izzie cracked up, but TJ rolled her eyes and went to look at a statue that looked just like the one we'd seen in the square earlier in the afternoon.

'The second copy of Michelangelo's *David*,' she said as she gazed up. 'These statues are so old. Don't you think they're impressive? Some were done in the fourteen hundreds, some in the fifteen.'

'Not exactly shy back, then, were they?' asked Izzie as we stared up at the statue of *Poseidon*, to the left of *David*.

'Not exactly well-endowed either,' said Nesta staring at the statue's willie. 'At least not in proportion to the rest of him.'

'Maybe the artists weren't allowed to make the willie big in the old days,' said TJ. 'I mean if it was in proportion to the rest of him, it would be enormous.'

This set us off laughing which attracted the attention of a group of Italian boys who came over to us.

'Bella occhi,' said one to Izzie.

'What did he say?' she asked Nesta.

'Shhh, I'm listening,' she whispered back.

The boys were burbling away in Italian and, even though I didn't understand any of it, I could tell by their expressions and body language that they were talking about us. What they didn't know was that Nesta understood. Having an Italian dad, she's been to Italy to visit his relatives here a few times and, though she says she doesn't speak the language fluently, she says she can make out what someone is saying. When they'd finished, she put her hand on her hip and said something to them in Italian. They scurried off like mice.

'What did you say?' I asked.

'I said that we were nuns and that our mother superior was watching from the other side of the square.'

'Brilliant,' I said.

'Shame,' said TJ. 'One of them was quite cute.'

For a short time, we sat on the side of a fountain by the statue of *Poseidon* and watched the world go by.

'The Italian women have such style,' said Nesta, as an elegant woman dressed in head-to-toe black walked past with a white husky dog. 'I think I'm going to dress in black from now on.'

I glanced over at the café where Mrs Elwes was. I could see her sitting at one of the outside tables and, like us, happily taking in the view.

'What's the time, Nesta?' I asked.

She glanced at her watch. 'Almost five.'

'Loads of time,' said TJ, who had been gazing up at a sombre-looking building with a tower behind and to the right of the fountain. 'Let's take a quick look in here.' She got up and soon disappeared into a door.

Izzie, Nesta and I wandered in after her and found ourselves in an elegant courtyard with pillars and stone steps leading upstairs.

TJ consulted her guidebook. 'This is the Palazzo Vecchio,' she said. 'It's where the Medici family lived in the fifteen hundreds.'

'Shall we take a look upstairs?' I asked, pointing at the steps.

'You have to pay to go in, I think,' said Nesta. She got out her purse and counted her euros.

'Still OK for time?' I asked.

Izzie glanced at her watch again. 'Loads.'

Nesta went over to the kiosk to enquire about entry. She turned back and gave us the thumbs up. 'Just got enough. Shall we do it?'

We nodded back at her.

Moments later we were up the stairs, exploring. The rooms were awesome, as all the walls and ceilings were covered with detailed paintings. Vast battle scenes in an enormous hall and seasonal country scenes in smaller rooms. There was something on every available surface and to see so much colour and design packed into one area was breathtaking.

'Maybe this is what they did instead of using wallpaper,' I said, as we reached yet another painted room and gazed out of the window over Florence. 'You know, you get a mate to come over and do a mural instead. It looks so ordinary from the outside but, inside, they must have spent millions doing all this.'

'Maybe we should do our rooms like this when we get back,' said Izzie. 'You know, paint scenes from our lives. Maybe not. I don't think my mum would be too pleased if I painted a pic of you lot over her posh Sanderson wallpaper.'

'She doesn't know what she's missing,' I said. 'I couldn't paint as well as this, but maybe I could see if any of Bandy Nelly's relatives are still alive and hire them to come over and do me a mural and a naked statue. Look lovely on the back patio with our garden gnomes and potted petunias.'

TJ gave me a look of despair. Sometimes I think she finds it hard that we don't all share her love of history.

From the window we could look out into the square, so I glanced over to the café to find Mrs Elwes. I couldn't see her.

'Can't see the teachers,' I said. 'What time is it? Maybe we'd better get going.'

'No,' said Nesta. 'We've only been in here about twenty minutes. We'll be fine.'

'It's about half five,' said Izzie.

'Is that all? I feel like we've been here ages,' I said.

Suddenly TJ slapped her forehead. 'Ohmigod,' she cried, then looked at her watch. 'Time. Did any of you guys put your clocks forward when we got off the plane?'

We all shook our heads. Then it dawned on me. 'Oh no,' I said. 'No wonder time seemed to be lasting forever. We're still on English time. Italy is an hour ahead. Remember Mrs Elwes told us to do it when we got off the plane.'

'Oh God! Yes, I remember,' said Izzie. 'We were too busy watching Lucy chat up the Teddy bear.'

We raced down the stairs, through the courtyard and across the square to the café. We scoured the customers sitting at the tables. No sigh of Mrs Elwes. No sign of Mr Johnson. No sign of any of the other girls in our class.

'Oh poo,' said Izzie.

'What do we do now?' asked Nesta.

'Get a cab,' I said. 'We know the name of the hotel.'

Nesta got her purse out and turned out the money in there. There were only a few notes left. 'No way is this enough.'

'Bus?' suggested TJ.

'There were a million at the station we passed. How would we know which one to get?' I asked.

'We could walk,' said Nesta. 'Does anyone remember the way back?'

Izzie, TJ and I shook our heads.

Stranded on our first day in Florence. A fine start to our holiday, I thought as I looked around and tried not to panic.

Chapter 10

Busking It

'When the going gets tough, the tough get going,' said Nesta.

'Meaning?' I asked.

'We come up with a solution,' said Nesta. 'It's not a problem. We'll find our own way back.'

'No,' said TJ. 'Phone. We ought to phone and let them know where we are.'

We looked around for a phone box. Not one in sight.

'Policeman,' I said.

We looked around for a policeman. Not one in sight.

'We could go and look for one,' suggested Izzie.

TJ shook her head. 'I don't think we should leave the square, in case one of the teachers is still looking for us.'

'Next great plan anybody?' asked Izzie.

'It's a sink or swim situation,' said TJ. 'I say we swim. We earn our cab fare.'

'And how exactly do you propose that we do that?' asked Izzie. 'Get a job? At this time of day?'

'When in Rome do as the Romans do,' said TJ.

'But this isn't Rome,' I said. 'It's Florence. What do you mean? Do as the Florentines do?'

'Mime,' said TJ and pointed over to where the Egyptian mummy had been only an hour earlier. 'Like the mummy. It can't be difficult.'

'Top idea,' said Nesta. She pulled off her woolly hat and gave it to TJ. 'OK, you go and stand in the square and us guys will keep an eye out for weirdos, as you won't be able to move your eyes when you get going.'

'But . . . but why me?' asked TJ. 'You'd be loads better at it.'

'Your idea,' said Nesta.

Izzie, Nesta and I went and sat back on the edge of the fountain while TJ positioned herself a few metres away with Nesta's hat in front of her. She made her body go rigid and positioned herself as though she were a dummy in a shop window with one arm out as though pointing and one leg slightly up. Not bad, I thought as the first group of tourists went past and stared at her. Then the Italian boys we'd met earlier spotted her and came over. They did everything they could to get her to react – waving their hands in front of her face, doing mad dances, one even started singing. TJ managed to keep a straight face until they all lined up in exactly the same posture as her. It was funny to watch and, in the end, TJ couldn't resist and started laughing.

Eventually the boys moved off, when they realised that TJ wasn't into being chatted up, and she went back into her pose. She stayed still for a good five minutes, but no one walked past. Then she started wobbling and almost fell over. She quickly resumed her position. Finally an old man with white hair passed by and dropped a few coins in front of her.

'Muchos gracias,' she said. The man gave her a strange look.

'That's Spanish,' called Nesta.

'I'm doing a Spanish mime,' TJ called back.

A few minutes later and she couldn't keep it up any longer. She dropped her posture and came over.

'It's *really* hard,' she said. 'My arms began to ache being in the same position for so long. It's like your muscles begin to shake. And it's boring, not so much keeping still but not being able to look around and move your eyes. One of you guys have a go.'

'Yeah, Nesta,' I said. 'Why don't you do something?'

'Like what?'

'Um . . . fortune-telling,' I said.

'No way,' said Nesta. 'I'm not a fortune-teller.'

'Oh come on. We need to get back to the hotel,' I said. 'I'm starving. Go on, try it. For us. Pleeeease. Just think, there's probably a lovely supper waiting for us and comfy beds and . . .'

'Lumpy pillows,' said Izzie.

'And two fuming teachers,' added TJ.

Izzie unwound her scarf from her neck and handed it to Nesta. 'Wrap this around your head. You are no longer Nesta. You are now Madam Rosa.'

'But it's you who's into all that heeby-jeeby, Iz. I don't know the first thing about it.'

'Ah,' said Izzie. 'But you're the only one of us that speaks any Italian, plus you are an actress. You don't know what parts you're going to have to play in your career. It will be good practice. Improvise. Say general things – the sort of things that will have happened to everybody, then you can't go wrong. Come on, I know you can do it.'

'Hmmm, I'm not so sure,' said Nesta, but she began to wind the scarf around her head like a turban. 'I don't think I should stand out in the square and do it. I'll sit at the end of the fountain near the pillar and you can send people to me. I'll tell you how to say, "Have your fortune told" in Italian.'

'Good idea,' said TJ.

While Nesta took up her position by a pillar, we called out what she'd told us to say into the square. *'Per la chiromante, da questa parte. Per la chiromante, da questa parte.'*

Most people walked by and looked at us as though we were mad, but a couple of women in their twenties came past and looked interested. One blonde, one brunette, they had backpacks on and looked like tourists.

'Per la chiromante, da questa parte,' I called to them, then decided to try it again in English. 'Fortune-telling, this way.'

'Oh fortune-telling,' said the blonde one in an Australian accent. She turned to her friend. 'How about it, Marie? See what the future has in store?'

Her friend laughed and looked over to where I was

pointing at Nesta. 'She doesn't look very old,' she said.

'Ah,' said Izzie, 'but she is from an ancient family of gypsies and has had the gift of seeing since birth. Age doesn't matter with the Oracle.'

Nice one, Iz, I thought as the women gave us ten euros and went over to Nesta. She really got into her part. She took the blonde woman's hand and then touched her cheek, looking deeply into her eyes. She then rolled her eyes up and swayed about. I thought she looked as though she was going to be sick, but I guess it was acting. And if there's one thing Nesta likes to do, that's act.

'You have travelled far . . .' she began in a deep husky voice.

Marie nodded.

'You are at a crossroad in your life . . .'

Again Marie nodded.

'You have known love . . . but you have also known pain . . .'

More enthusiastic nods.

'I see a tall, dark man . . .'

Marie looked up at her friend. 'Ian,' she said.

Nesta nodded. 'I see good things . . . a bright future . . .'

Marie's friend grinned. This was obviously what they wanted to hear.

'I see many children . . .'

At this Marie's face crumpled and she burst into tears and rushed off. Nesta looked shocked. 'What's the matter? What did I say?'

Her friend looked dismayed. 'We came on holiday because

she found out that she can never have children. She's worried her boyfriend Ian wants them and will choose someone else that can give him them. What you've just said confirms it.'

With that, the lady rushed off to join her friend.

'Oops,' said Izzie. 'OK. Cut that out of the act. Too risky. Don't mention babies. Talk about love, marriage and that sort of thing.'

'Per la chiromante, da questa parte,' TJ called out to two elegantly dressed men who strolled by. *'Per la chiromante, da questa parte.* Fortunes told in English and Italian.'

'Go ahead, Ryan,' said one in an American accent. 'It would be fun.'

'Why not?' said the blond one and TJ led him to Nesta.

Nesta looked at his hand and into his eyes. 'You are a very handsome man,' she said. 'I see much love in your life.'

Ryan turned and grinned up at his friend.

'I see a blonde girl. I see love. I see marriage . . .'

The expression on Ryan's friends face turned cold. 'Blonde girl?' he asked. 'What does she look like exactly?'

'Um. Very pretty. Um. Very nice lady,' said Nesta.

'I knew it . . .' said the friend and, before we knew it, he had stormed off.

'*Now* what?' I asked nobody in particular.

'Wh . . . what did I say?' asked Nesta.

Ryan sighed and ran to catch up with his friend.

Nesta shrugged. 'What was the problem?'

'Obvious, you dingbat,' said Izzie. 'They're gay and now,

thanks to you, one of them thinks the other has got something going with a pretty, blonde girl.'

We looked over to the other side of the square where we could see the two men having a row.

'Oops,' said Nesta. 'I guess this wasn't such a good idea after all. Fortune-telling isn't as easy as it looks.' She unwound the scarf from her head and gave it back to Izzie. 'So Lucy . . .'

All three of them turned and looked at me.

'What?' I asked.

'Your go,' said Izzie.

'I can't do anything. I can't sing, can't act. Only thing I can do is make clothes and that's not really an option.' I said.

'And we need some more money to get back to the hotel,' said Nesta.

'Try the mime thing,' said TJ. 'A cab can't cost that much. We probably only need a few more euros. Someone might take pity on you.'

'Thanks a lot,' I said, but I knew there was no getting out of it. We were mates and I couldn't let them down.

I went into the middle of the square and tried to copy the pose of one of the statues near the Uffizi with my arms reaching up in the air, legs slightly crossed. I stood as still as I could, eyes fixed upwards.

I could hear the girls cracking up laughing behind me. Not fair, I thought. I didn't laugh at them. I was vaguely aware of someone standing in front of me, but I kept my eyes fixed skywards. I didn't want to ruin my pose by looking at whoever was there.

'You OK?' asked a familiar American voice.

I let myself look ahead. It was Teddy standing there with an amused grin on his face.

'I was doing mime.'

'Mime? Oh right. OK,' he said. 'I thought you looked kind of uncomfortable. Like you needed the bathroom.'

I felt myself blush scarlet. So much for my career as a mime artist, I thought.

'Oh God,' I heard Izzie say behind me. 'Here comes trouble.'

'Lucy Lovering!' cried a voice to my left. 'Izzie Foster! Nesta Williams. TJ WATTS!'

We turned to see Mr Johnson advancing towards us. He was smoking a cigarette and had a face like thunder.

Things to Do if You Get Stranded With No Dosh

Pray
Cry
Beg
Busk
Sing
Do a mime act

Slightly more sensible options are:

Call someone you know and reverse the charges (preferably someone in the same country!).
Get a cab to someone or somewhere you know. Get them to pay the cab fare at their end, then settle up with them later.
Ask a police officer for help. (But make sure he is a policeman and not someone *miming* being a police officer, as you never know.)

Chapter 11

International Woman of Mystery

'I'm going to be an international woman of experience and sophistication,' I announced the next morning.

'Me too,' said TJ through a mouthful of the sponge cake that was served for breakfast. I'd wanted my usual toast or muesli, but it wasn't on offer on the buffet table. There was cake, ham, cheese, tomatoes, croissants, tinned pears, prunes and yogurt – nothing I fancied in the morning so I made do with a roll.

'And what exactly does that entail?' asked Izzie.

'It entails travelling a lot, staying in the best hotels,' I said, 'knowing all about art and culture, having love affairs with interesting, talented men and looking divine at every occasion.'

'OK,' said Izzie. 'I'll be one as well, then. Nesta you in?'

'I already am one,' said Nesta, who was wearing sunglasses even though we were indoors. She'd borrowed them from her mum especially for the trip. Big, black Gucci ones. They looked fab.

'I see Mr Johnson has abandoned his no-smoking resolution,' said Izzie with a sideways glance at the table where he was sitting and puffing away. At least he seemed in a better mood this morning. He'd been hopping mad the previous night, even though we'd done our best grovel act and tried to explain about the time difference and how we'd forgotten to put our watches forward. Apparently he thought we'd wandered off and had gone looking for us in the adjacent squares. Before he calmed down, he threatened to put us on the next plane back to England, but then he must have realised that it wasn't such a great idea as either he or Mrs Elwes would have had to go with us, leaving the rest of the group with only one teacher.

Our journey back to the hotel had turned into a bit of a farce, as at first Teddy had offered to give us all a lift in the limo, which of course Mr Johnson refused. 'We'll get a cab,' he said loftily and ushered us away. Only there were no cabs and, after traipsing around for half an hour, who drove past, but Teddy, who offered us a ride again. This time Mr Johnson gave in and so we drove back in style. Teddy seemed really nice. I sat next to him and got chatting while the others tried to calm Mr Johnson down. Teddy said he came over at least once a year, usually in the summer holidays, to visit his dad in Milan, but had been allowed time out of school to attend his grandmother's funeral. His parents were divorced and he lived in the States with his mum and he didn't see his dad's side of the family very much. His dad remarried and worked in textiles and had factories all over Italy. I told him that I wanted to be a fashion designer and he promised to show me some of his dad's fabric samples. He asked where we were going sightseeing and, when I told him that we'd be going to the Duomo the next morning, he'd said he might see me up there. He wanted to take some photos from the top for an album he was making in memory of his grandmother's life and where she'd lived.

When I was lying in bed later, going over the day, I decided that I'd like to get to know him better. As Florence was so different to North London, he was different to the boys I met back home. I wanted to be open to new experiences on all levels and it wouldn't hurt to broaden my horizons on the boy front as well as seeing a new country. Besides, I was only in Italy for a week, too short a time for things to get complicated. No harm in just getting to know him.

As we resumed our sightseeing after breakfast, it was obvious we were in the doghouse with Mr Johnson and Mrs Elwes, who insisted on keeping us within their sight. I hadn't envisaged having two teachers on my tail as part of my new role as international woman of sophistication and experience, but I didn't mind too much as there was so much to see and Mrs Elwes was a great tour guide. First we did the Uffizi Gallery with a million other tourists and school parties on half-term, so it was difficult to see anything in the long corridors and rooms there. It was easier for the others as they're tall but, when you're short like me and there are twenty people crowding round a painting or piece of sculpture, it's hard to see over their heads. I found myself only getting glimpses of the art on display in between people's armpits. TJ was in heaven as she loves history and we had to drag her away from some of the rooms. Nesta and Izzie seemed more interested in taking in what the tourists were wearing and eyeing up boys than becoming experts on Renaissance art.

After the Uffizi, we explored the interior of the Duomo, which was awesome. The domed ceiling was painted with some very strange-looking paintings. Some of heaven, which were OK, but the ones of hell were seriously gruesome. People being swallowed head first by demons or having their limbs or heads cut off. Yuck. Not my idea of spiritually uplifting. I began to feel a tingle of excitement at the prospect of seeing Teddy again, though. This is a new chapter in my book of life, I thought as we wandered round the vast cathedral. My cosy life in North London seemed a million miles away. Tony seemed a million miles away. Teddy, on the other hand, might only be a few steps away at the top of the Duomo.

At the end of the tour of the interior, Mrs Elwes called us all over to her. 'For those of you who want to go to the top, you're free to do so. There is a fantastic view from up there, so join the queue if you wish to go up. Mr Johnson will be at the back of the group and I'll stay down here to meet you on your return.'

'Well, I want to go,' said TJ.

'And we all know that Lucy will,' said Nesta. 'Isn't that where you said you'd meet Teddy?'

I nodded. 'If he's there. We didn't say an exact time.'

I got out my mirror and applied a slick of lip-gloss, then we went outside to join the long queue that wound itself halfway around the side of the Duomo. After about fifteen minutes, we were inside again and being directed to a small door where we could see stone steps leading upwards. I really hoped that Teddy would be at the top when we got there. It would be so romantic, like Meg Ryan meeting Tom Hanks up on top of the Empire State Building in the movie *Sleepless in Seattle*. Only this is Italy. And there's no lift up.

'Last one to the top's a sissy,' said Izzie as she sprinted up the first spiral of steps.

We raced after her and kept up a good pace for about five minutes, after which we had to stop and catch our breath. The stairway was very narrow, going round and round and round and *round*. I felt myself getting dizzy and Nesta was feeling the same.

'Don't know if I can do this,' she said. 'My head's spinning.'

We looked behind us, but there was no way we could turn back as the stairway was too narrow and already we could see the next lot of tourists coming up behind us.

'This has to be what hell is like,' said Izzie as we set off again. 'Stuck on a tiny stairway for ever with a million people behind you pushing you upwards so that you can't rest.'

'No, we can do it,' said TJ. 'We're young, we're fit . . .'

'We're gonna die . . .' said Nesta as she puffed her way ahead.

On and up and on and up and *on* and *up* we trudged.

'We have to be almost there,' I said, after what seemed like an eternity of climbing.

Suddenly the stair opened out to a small landing and we could see people coming down.

A boy with his mother went past us and grinned. 'You're about halfway up,' he said.

'Oh noooooo,' groaned Izzie. 'I thought this trip was supposed to be fun. This is a nightmare.'

We made our way up more steps and more steps and more steps. By now, no one was speaking. It took up too much energy. It must be about five hundred steps to the top, I thought as I stopped for a moment to catch my breath. Now I understood why Mrs Elwes hadn't wanted to accompany us. She must have done it before and knew what was involved. I hope Teddy's not up there, I thought. I might have looked OK when I was down at the bottom, but I could feel that my face was now scarlet and I was out of breath and sweating like mad. Not my most alluring look. As I panted my way up, suddenly there was an opening and a ladder, and I prayed that this might be the end of the steps. Izzie went up the ladder first, then TJ, then Nesta, then me. Then at last, we were at the top and Florence stretched out in front of us. It was an amazing view and, as it was a bright day, we could see for miles. It felt like we were on the top of the world looking out. I edged my way over to the metal barrier to look down.

'Woah,' I said, stepping back quickly. We were very high up and people on the streets down below looked like ants. Everything went blurry and, I felt as if I was going to fall. 'Don't go to the edge.'

Izzie stepped forward and like me, quickly stepped back. 'High! ET wants to go home. Don't like it.'

'You big bunch of girls,' said TJ, who was happy close to the edge and looking over. 'Let's walk round.'

I followed her along the narrow landing around the top, but I made sure that I kept as far away from the barriers as possible. Even though they were waist-high, I didn't feel comfortable at all.

There were about a hundred people up there and I quickly scanned them to see if I could see Teddy, but there didn't seem to be any sign of him.

'He's not here, is he?' asked Izzie as she too scanned the crowd.

I shrugged. 'Well I guess it was a bit of a long shot as he might have come earlier.' I did feel disappointed though. It would have been great to have seen him up here at such a great location. And, with a bit of luck, he could have carried me back down.

After lunch of ciabatta, mozzarella and tomatoes in a café near the Duomo, our bus took us back up to the Piazza Michelangelo, the square with the statue of *David* and his bum that we'd been to the day before. We got off the bus to explore the market stalls there, where everyone bought aprons with a picture of the torso of the statue of *David* on them. I bought six as I thought they'd make fun presents and they were only eight euros each. The aprons were hysterical as they showed David's willie and all the girls on our tour put them on and lined up for a photo in front of the statue. Sadly, Mr Johnson didn't seem to find it very funny, especially when Nesta tried to get him to wear one. After the market stalls, we went up to a church and a fabulous old cemetery to the right of the square. Some of the gravestones were like works of art, with statues of people and ornate sculptures of flowers and swords. Of course we all had to have our pictures taken pretending to be angels standing over the graves.

At about three in the afternoon, Mrs Elwes announced that we were allowed an hour to explore or have a coffee or just relax.

'And you girls,' she said, looking at Izzie, TJ, Nesta and me, 'what time do you have on your watches?'

'Three, Mrs Elwes,' said TJ. 'We've put our watches on the right time.'

'And don't forget we have our mobiles,' said Nesta. 'My dad had them upgraded for us to use in Europe as a holiday present.'

'Switched on?'

'Yes.'

'OK, I've got the numbers so I'll give you a second chance to go off and explore but, if you're not back in an hour, you're in *deep* trouble. Understood?'

'Understood,' said Izzie.

As soon as she'd wandered off a short distance, Nesta turned to the rest of us.

'Hotel Villa Corelli,' she said. 'It's only down the road. Remember, we saw it from the bus.'

'But we can't go in there,' said TJ. 'We're not guests.'

'No problem,' said Nesta. 'Just walk in like you own the place. No one will ask. Remember Mrs Elwes said she went for cocktails? We'll have a Coke and, anyway, we know Teddy. We can say we're visiting him if anyone asks. Oh come on, TJ. I've always wanted to look in one of those really swanky hotels.'

Normally I'd agree with TJ. I'm not very brave about going in very posh places as I feel intimidated, but Florence was having a weird effect on me and I felt like I wanted to try everything and no one was going to stop me. Plus, if I was going to be an international woman of experience, I needed to have some. Experiences, that is.

'And maybe we'll see Teddy again,' said Nesta. 'It's important for Lucy to help her get over my dumb brother.'

'Lead the way,' said Izzie.

'It's neoclassic,' said TJ as we walked up towards the hotel's entrance.

'Neo-posh,' said Izzie as we walked inside.

Even Nesta was fazed when we walked into the hotel lobby. It was fabulous with a very distinctive smell. Money. Marbled floors, marbled walls, humungous displays of exotic flowers. No one was about and it was clearly not a place where four teenage girls could hang about without looking conspicuous. And no way was it a place that you could just pop into for a Coke. The others were about to turn away, when I took a deep breath and marched straight up to the reception desk and rang the bell. A moment later, a blonde lady appeared from a back room.

'Er . . . excuse me. Do you speak English?'

'Yes, madam. How can I help?'

'We're here to see Teddy Ambrosini Junior, please.'

'Just a moment,' she said. 'Who should I say is calling?'

'Lucy Lovering. Um. Junior.'

She gave me a funny look, then went to her phone and dialled. A few moments later she glanced up. 'He's coming down,' she said.

'Cool,' I said. 'I mean, thanks.'

Five minutes later, Teddy appeared in the lobby. He looked delighted to see us all.

'Hey,' he said. 'I'm so sorry I couldn't make the Duomo this morning. My aunt turned up to check I was OK.'

'Why are you staying here,' asked Nesta, 'if you're family lives in Florence?'

'They don't,' said Teddy. 'That is, some of them do. My dad has a place in Milan. It was my grandmother who lived in Florence, and her place is packed out with assorted relatives so Dad thought I'd be more comfortable here.'

'I'll say,' said Nesta.

'We're very sorry to hear about her death,' said Izzie. 'Were you close to her?'

Teddy shook his head. 'Yeah. She was a great lady. I didn't see as much of her as my American grandmother, but I used to see her once a year when I was over visiting Dad. He's arriving tonight with my stepmother. Say, would you like to see my room?'

We all nodded and trooped after him up a flight of stairs and into a room on the first floor. I say room, but it was more like a suite. It must cost a bomb to stay here, I thought as I took in the richly coloured rugs on the floor and heavy drapes at the window.

'Nice place,' said TJ.

'It used to be a private residence,' said Teddy. 'Royal folks' pad.'

'Cool,' said TJ.

'I was just putting some photos on the computer,' said Teddy, 'ready to send back home to my mom.'

'Brilliant,' I said. 'Can we see?'

We all crowded round the laptop, which was set up on a writing desk. Teddy pressed a button on his keypad and lines of photographs appeared.

'God, I wish I could send photos,' said Nesta. 'I'd love to send pics home.'

'I can do that for you,' said Teddy and reached over to his camera.

We spent the next fifteen minutes larking about and taking pictures. Izzie in a Buddha pose on the bed. Nesta sprawled like Cleopatra over the bed with her sunglasses on and a glass in her hand. Me peeping out from behind one of the curtains. Izzie insisted that I had one taken with Teddy, and it all got a bit silly as he pulled a rose out of an arrangement on top of the TV and knelt on the floor and held it up to me. Course, I went red and grinned like an idiot.

‘*Romeo and Juliet*,’ said Nesta.

‘Only that was in Verona, not Florence,’ said TJ.

‘Who cares?’ said Nesta. ‘Verona, Florence. It’s all Italy and it’s all romantic.’

It didn’t take Teddy long to transfer the pictures on to the computer, take down our e-mail addresses then, with a ping, send them off to our computers in England.

‘The Renaissance folk might have been whizzes at art,’ said TJ, ‘but we have digital cameras and e-mail.’

After cups of tea in delicate china, we took our leave and ran back up the hill to the square. We didn’t want to be in trouble with Mrs Elwes and only just made it in time.

‘You going to see him again?’ asked TJ as we got back on the bus.

I nodded. Before we’d left, Teddy had asked for our itinerary, so I’d given him a rough idea of where we’d be going in the next few days in case he could get time off from his family duties. I felt brilliant. This place may be full of art and history and fantastic stories of who’d lived here in past times, I thought, but the past has gone. I’m here now. I’m alive and my story’s still unfolding.

Back at our hotel, we had supper and a bit of a laugh with the boys from the other school, then went back to our rooms and got into our pyjamas. We raided the minibar for goodies – one bar of chocolate, two chunks each. We tried watching the telly, but it was all in Italian so we decided to phone home. We took turns and Nesta was last to go.

She put the phone down and sighed.

'What?' asked Izzie.

'I should have thought . . .'

'What?' asked Izzie again.

'We share our Inbox back home. Tony saw the photographs.'

'So?' asked Izzie.

'The one of Lucy and Teddy. Mum said he flipped and stormed out of the flat.'

'Serves him right,' said Izzie. 'I mean, it was him that finished with her and all because she wouldn't have sex with him.'

'It wasn't just that . . .' I began to protest.

'Apparently he came back later,' continued Nesta, 'packed his rucksack and said he was going off to some rave in Devon.'

'So?' asked TJ.

Nesta glanced at me. 'With Andrea Morton,' she said.

'Who's she?' asked TJ.

'You don't want to know,' said Nesta.

'I do,' I said.

Nesta sighed. 'Andrea Morton's this girl who's been after him for ages. I didn't say anything about her before, Lucy, because, for one thing, he was smitten with you and, for another, he didn't seem interested. She was doing all the chasing.'

'How old is she?' asked Izzie.

'Seventeen,' said Nesta. 'Why?'

'Obvious, isn't it?'

'No.'

'Seventeen. Legal. We all know what Tony wants,' said Izzie.

Nesta lay back on her bed. 'Well, good luck to him.'

'Exactly,' I said. I felt a twinge of jealousy, but I knew that he'd move on sooner or later. He had to. I couldn't expect him to stay single just because we'd split up. I mustn't mind, I told myself. I have to move on as well and I knew just the person I wanted to do that with.

'Um. Do you think that room service will deliver chocolate?' asked Izzie, who was on her knees on the floor with her face in the minibar. 'We're all out here.'

'Yeah,' said TJ. 'Who needs boys when you can have chocolate?'

'Ah, but maybe we do need them when we *haven't* any,' said Nesta. 'Let's call the boys in their rooms. Maybe they haven't eaten their supplies.'

There are four hundred and sixty-three steps to the top of the Duomo.

Take water and sandwiches. And oxygen.

Chapter 12

Exploring

'Maybe Teddy's gay,' said Izzie as we got ready for bed on Thursday evening.

'Maybe,' I said, 'or maybe he's just come out of a relationship and is off girls for a while.'

'No way,' said Nesta. 'I've seen the way he looks at you and I'm never wrong about these things. He fancies you big time.'

'So why hasn't he kissed me, then?'

I'd seen Teddy every day since Sunday in his hotel. I got the feeling he was a bit lonely as, although his dad and stepmother had arrived to join him at the hotel, once the funeral was over, his dad left Teddy to his own devices as he had business in Florence to attend to and his stepmother wanted to go shopping. He came over in the evenings for an hour or so and we sat in the lounge downstairs and chatted. We found we had loads in common as he was interested in design and wanted to do it when he went to college, though he wasn't sure whether to do furniture or fabric. He brought samples of his dad's fabrics for me to look at and they were stunning, all the vibrant colours of Italy. At the end of the evening, I'd walk him back to the limo, which always waited for him in the car park.

As the week had gone on, I could tell he liked me, but he never made a move, not even to hold my hand, and I began to wonder if he liked me only as a friend; if there was something wrong with me or I'd misread the signals. All the other girls from our school were having a whale of a time and just about everyone had got off with someone.

Izzie spent every moment she could with Jay and it looked like they were getting serious. TJ hung out with Liam, although she said it was platonic as she didn't fancy him. He did look a bit odd, as one of the boys in their group had shaved off one of his eyebrows when he was asleep on the first night in Italy as a joke. Not a great look. Nesta however, for the first time ever, was having a hard time pulling. Loads of boys on the school tour fancied her, but she'd set her sights higher. She fancied Marco, one of the waiters. He was well fit. Tall and dark with deep brown eyes. She found out from one of the other waiters who spoke good English that Marco was a musician who was working at the hotel part-time. Sadly though, no matter how hard she flirted, he played it cool and treated her as though she was one of his customers. Nothing more. Of course that only made him more attractive in Nesta's eyes, and it could only be a matter of time before he succumbed as Nesta, like her brother, liked a challenge.

And then there was me. Every day at breakfast, Chris, the boy who'd given me the eye on the plane, sauntered past and made some stupid comment or tried to get my attention by throwing bits of croissant at me. Not a very impressive way of getting attention in my book. No way was I interested in him. I liked Teddy, but I wasn't sure what was happening with him. I thought he fancied me, but nothing. Not even a peck on the cheek. It was weird. After all the anxiety about Tony trying it on all the time, now I was worried about a boy who didn't want to try at all. I tried to tell myself that it didn't matter. Nothing could come of it anyway and I'd had a brilliant week exploring some of the places around Florence with the school.

We'd spent Monday touring the churches and palaces in Florence, and then on Tuesday we'd been out to Siena which is a medieval town built on three hills. Nesta got in trouble there as it was an unusually warm day for the time of year and she went into one of the churches in a tiny tank top. The man on duty gave her a filthy look, then handed her a sort of paper pinny to wear to cover herself up. Course, she had to have her photo taken in front of one of the churches with it over her head like a mad nun. The place I liked the best there was the Piazza del Campo. It's a huge square built on a slope in the middle of the town and, twice a year, they hold a famous horse race there called the *Palio*. Horses race round the outside of the square while up to thirty thousand people stand in the middle to watch. Don't think I'd like to be there for that. I'd get squashed and wouldn't see a thing.

On Wednesday we visited Lucca, which was a lovely quiet place. It's surrounded by a high wall and you can only get in through one of six enormous gates. Inside, people tend to get about by bicycle as cars aren't allowed, and we hired bikes and rode round the track on top of the city wall. It was a great way to see it all and much more relaxing than Siena which was hard work because, being on a hill, some of the streets were very steep. The bike ride also made a nice change from yet another church. They were beginning to blur in my head and I couldn't remember which church or cathedral was where.

My favourite trip was to a place called San Gimignano on Thursday morning, and it was there that I felt like I'd really fallen in love with Italy. Like Lucca, cars weren't allowed in and the only way in was through one of two great gates in a ginormous wall. TJ told me that it was nicknamed the Medieval Manhattan because there were thirteen towers there, and that there used to be seventy towers in the old days. Apparently people used to build them to show that they were rich and successful. The higher the tower, the richer you were. It was smaller than Siena and Lucca and only had two squares, but I really liked the atmosphere. You could really imagine how it must have been in the past. Narrow streets lined with shops led to the main squares and, in one of them, there was a lovely church with stunning frescoes. TJ told me that some of the movie *Tea With Mussolini* had been filmed in there. We went up a tower in the centre of the town and from there was the most wonderful view of the Tuscan countryside. San Gimignano is on a hill so we were high up before we ascended the tower but, once up, we could see for miles in all directions. Rolling green hills, cyprus trees stretched out in front of us with the occasional dot of a farm or villa. It looked magical, like a painting. I felt as though I was standing on the threshold of my whole life, looking out on the beginning of endless possibilities. I really, really want to travel, I decided. See as much as I can while I can.

'I'm totally frescoed out,' said Izzie, as we travelled back from our Friday trip to a winery and yet another church on the outskirts of Florence.

'Me too,' said Nesta. 'I've got art coming out of my ears.'

'Yeah right,' I said, laughing. I hadn't noticed Nesta or Izzie taking too much notice of the art as we visited places. The boys from our hotel had done all the same tours as us and they'd spent all the time they could hanging out with them.

As we got off the coach, Mrs Elwes announced that we were to be allowed an evening out on our own as long as we stayed in groups.

'Call Teddy and let him know,' said Nesta. 'We can all go out. We'll cover for you as Mrs Elwes and Mr Johnson will think that you're with us.'

'I want to go out with Jay,' said Izzie, 'so can you cover for me too?'

'No prob,' said Nesta. 'TJ and I had planned to hang out with the boys anyway. We can say we were all together.'

Half an hour later, the girls escorted me to the Ponte Vecchio, the bridge where I had arranged to meet Teddy.

He was already waiting for me when I arrived and I agreed to meet the girls back there after two hours.

At first, it felt strange to be on my own with him, wandering round unfamiliar streets in the dark and there wasn't a whole lot to see as the shops were closed. After a while, he asked if I'd like to drive around some of the surrounding area. I nodded. Even though I'd only known him under a week, I could tell that he was trustworthy. Besides the girls knew where he was staying and had my mobile number, if he decided to kidnap me and sell me to the slave trade.

As we sat back in the leather seats in the limo, I longed to reach out and hold his hand, but I didn't want to seem forward and I certainly didn't want to feel an idiot if he wasn't into it. The driver drove us out of Florence and up to a little town called Fiesole in one of the hills, where we got out and strolled along the lanes until we came to some steps. At the top of the steps, we sat on the wall and gazed out over the lights of Florence, twinkling away in the distance. He stood behind me and, for a moment, I thought he was going to put his arms round me. But he didn't. It was beginning to drive me mad. I wondered if Izzie was right and he was gay. He did seem like a sensitive person and he dressed beautifully, in simple but well-cut clothes, the way a lot of gay people do.

'Have you seen that film *A Room With a View*?' he asked.

'Yes. I saw it before I came out here.' I had a quick flash of the night I'd watched it, wrapped in Tony's arms before he got his attack of the wandering hands. For a moment, I felt sad and wished he was here with me looking out at the view, standing behind me and snuggling into my neck.

'And do you remember the scene where Helena Bonham Carter's character is in the poppy field and sees the boy she likes?'

'I do.' It was a really romantic scene – probably what got Tony going, I thought.

'It was up here that it was filmed,' said Teddy and at last he put his arms round me. 'Do you remember the name of the character that Helena Bonham Carter played?' he asked as he turned me round to face him.

I shook my head. 'No.'

Teddy smiled. 'It was Lucy. Her first time in Florence. The film was in the classic collection on the plane coming over here, so I thought I'd give it a watch seeing as it was set here. Then the first girl I meet when I get off the plane is called Lucy. Her first time in Florence. Kind of like fate or synchronicity or something.' And then he kissed me.

After a few moments he leaned back. 'I've been wanting to do that all week but, bit mad I know, I wanted to wait until I could bring you up here. Even though it was a sunny day in the movie and it's dark now, I wanted our first kiss to be up here just like the movie.'

I felt really touched. It was the most romantic thing anyone had ever done for me. Tony may have got the DVD out for me, but wanting to play out a scene from it in exactly the same location, that's cool. For a moment, I felt sad that it wasn't Tony that I was sharing a kiss with, then I made myself focus back on the present. Tony's moved on, I told myself. He's doing God knows what with Andrea Morton in Devon. It's over between us and I mustn't let memories of him ruin what could be a perfect moment with someone new. Teddy wrapped me in his arms again and I snuggled in and pushed any thoughts of Tony away.

'So what about the second kiss?' I asked. 'Where should that be?'

'Anywhere you like,' he said with a smile.

So we kissed in the lane going back to the square, in the square, in the car driving back into Florence and again on the Ponte Vecchio. He was a really good kisser and I felt like I was in a movie. Maybe not *A Room With a View* as that was about Edwardian times, but it felt every bit as special.

By the time the girls came to collect me, I felt as though I was floating on air.

A Room With a View (1985)

Directed by James Ivory
Written by Ruth Prawer Jhabvala
Based on the book by EM Forster
Starring: Helena Bonham Carter,
Julian Sands, Simon Callow
Denholm Elliott, Maggie Smith,
Daniel Day-Lewis, Judi Dench

Chapter 13

Outsider

'I've heard of love making you feel weird,' said Nesta as I retched into the loo the following morning, 'but this is taking it a bit far.'

'Oh ha ha,' I said weakly as another spasm of nausea hit my stomach.

'Must have been that seafood pizza you had last night on the way back from the bridge,' said Izzie as she leaned over the sink and soaked a flannel. 'I told you you should have had the four cheeses.'

The mention of food brought on a fresh wave of sickness and I had to bend over the loo again. This is not the view I had in mind when I came to Italy and certainly not how I envisaged spending my last day, I thought as I gazed at the white bowl beneath me.

'Don't . . . talk . . . about . . . food . . .' I groaned.

'I'll go and get Mrs Elwes,' said TJ, offering me a glass of water while Izzie put the wet flannel on my forehead.

Food poisoning, Mrs Elwes declared fifteen minutes later and I was put to bed with some tablets for my stomach and strict instructions not to get out of bed.

Izzie put her coat on ready for the trip. 'I'm so sorry you'll miss Pisa,' she said.

I felt myself wanting to retch again. 'Ugh. Please. Don't mention pizza.'

'No. Pisa. Pisa, where we're going today,' said Izzie.

I waved her away. 'Pisa, pizza, whatever. I never want to see food again.'

I was hardly aware of the girls slipping out of the room and I must have dozed off as, the next thing I knew, it was eleven o'clock and I was alone in the room. I lay there for a while staring at the paint peeling off the ceiling, then climbed off the bunk and tried standing up. I definitely felt better. I looked at myself in the wardrobe mirror. A little pale, but it seemed like the worst of the sickness had passed. I climbed onto Nesta's bed, lay down and flicked on the TV, but it was all in Italian. I attempted to have a shower, but the water was freezing. I tried to read, but it seemed like a waste to be in bed when I was on holiday so I decided to explore the hotel and see if anyone was about. The corridors were empty and the only sound was the hoover behind closed doors. Cleaning ladies were busy in the lounge, so no chance of hanging out there. In the end, I decided to go back to my room and call Teddy and see if he was free to act out more scenes from *A Room With a View.*

He wasn't in his hotel so I tried his mobile.

'Come and join me,' he said after I'd explained why I wasn't in Pisa with the others. 'I'm at the station waiting to meet my stepsisters, Arianna and Cecilia. They're on the train from Milan and I promised Dad that I'd meet them.'

'You didn't say you had sisters.'

'They're not my dad's. Not blood sisters. They're my stepmother's kids from her previous marriage.'

'Are you sure I won't be in the way?'

'Course not. You'll like them. I'll send the car for you.'

When I got out of the limo at the station, I began to feel ill again and wondered if going out had been a good idea. The station was heaving with people, dashing to get their train or meeting passengers. It felt overwhelming. I was about to turn back to the limo when I spotted Teddy by the ticket office.

'Train should have been in ten minutes ago, but it was delayed,' he said, as he took my arm and he led me towards the platforms. 'Should be here in a moment though.'

I started to feel faint being among so many people who were all in a hurry and for a moment felt like I was going to fall over.

'I'll sit back here,' I said as I spied a bench, 'and catch you up in a moment.'

'Sure you're OK?' asked Teddy. 'You look kind of green.'

I nodded. 'It's the new fashion. Green is the new black. I'll be OK. Go. You don't want to miss your stepsisters.'

I watched him make his way over to the platform as a train

came in and, as its doors opened, people started spilling out on to the platform. I looked among them for two young girls, but couldn't see any that were unaccompanied. Then I realised that he hadn't told me how old they were. Maybe they were older than him.

A couple of blonde girls in jeans wandered down the platform. They walked straight past Teddy, so not them. Then a very fat girl and her skinny friend with frizzy hair, but no, not them. Then, oh no, I thought, as two stunning girls in tip-to-toe black got off the train. Hope it's not them. They're way too glamorous and I feel such a mess. They walked past Teddy, although one turned back to check him out. But no, not them. I felt a sigh of relief. Suddenly I heard someone call out Teddy's name and he waved. Coming towards him were two tall girls who looked about eighteen. If the two previous girls had been stunning, these two were super stunning. As in mega. They looked like they'd just walked off the pages of one of my Italian *Vogue* magazines. One of them had wild, curly black hair almost down to her waist. She was wearing a pair of black jeans (with diamanté down the seams – it looked as if she had sprayed them on) and the highest pair of pointy boots I'd ever seen. Men were turning their heads to look at her. She kissed Teddy on both cheeks and he grinned back at her. The other girl held back a moment, then took her turn at the two kisses. She was classically beautiful with fabulous cheekbones and silver-blond hair pulled back in a high ponytail. Like her sister, she had high pointy boots on. It was hard to tell which was the oldest as they both looked so grown-up and self-assured.

'Hey, I want you to meet someone,' said Teddy, beckoning me to come forward. I stood up and shakily walked towards them. I felt like a midget peasant in my scruffy trainers, baggy jeans and unwashed hair. The girls towered over me and looked at Teddy quizzically.

'Arianna, Cecilia, this is Lucy,' he said. 'She's . . .' He grinned at me. 'What are you? A friend of mine. Yeah. She's here on a school trip from England.'

'Oh how fantastic,' said Arianna, the dark-haired one. 'You're English. I *love* the English. Where are you from?'

'London.' I felt tiny compared to her. Pale. Uninteresting.

'I know London well,' continued Arianna. 'Chelsea. Kensington. Mayfair. And Harvey Nichols. I love it. And the hotel we stayed in was divine. So quaint. Browns. You know it?'

I shook my head.

'Which part do you live in?' she asked.

'Muswell Hill.'

She looked at her sister who shrugged.

'Muswell Hill?' asked Cecilia. 'Where's that?'

'In the north.'

'Ah. We didn't go there.' Arianna put her arm through mine. 'So you come with us back to the hotel? We can talk all about England.'

They plied Teddy with their luggage and he grinned sheepishly at me as the girls pulled him away towards the exit where the driver was waiting to take the bags.

I trotted along with them, feeling more and more like a child who was with grown-ups.

Once in the car, the girls began chatting away in Italian to Teddy. Just as they had perfect English accents when they spoke to me, he seemed to have a perfect Italian one when he spoke to them. I decided to make an effort to join in.

'You speak great English,' I said to the girls. 'And you speak great Italian,' I said to Teddy. 'Do you speak other languages?'

'French, German . . .' said Arianna.

'Spanish and a little Russian,' said Cecilia. 'How about you?'

I was beginning to feel more and more inadequate and wished I hadn't asked. 'Um. Double Dutch,' I offered.

The girls looked at me with a puzzled expression.

'She's joking,' said Teddy. 'It's like slang.'

'Oh, OK. Double Dutch. Cool,' said Arianna.

'You speak Italian?' asked Cecilia.

'A little . . .' I said, praying that she wouldn't ask me to say anything. 'Where's the loo?' was about as much as I'd learned.

'But how rude of us,' said Arianna. 'Speaking in Italian. We must speak English.'

She's a nice girl, I thought. She can see that I can't understand a word of what they were saying in Italian and is trying to include me. Beautiful *and* nice *and* sophisticated *and* speaks a load of languages. As they chatted about England in an attempt to include me, I realised that the England they knew was not the same as the England I inhabited. Private schools. Private cinemas. Private parties. Polo matches in Windsor. Ascot. Restaurants I'd never heard of. They were like the girls Nesta met when she went out with a rich boy last year. Girls who move in different circles. Circles with lots of money. I felt like a complete outsider and at a loss for anything to say. Asking if they knew Marks and Spencer on the Broadway in Muswell Hill just wasn't an option.

This isn't good, I thought, I feel excluded when they speak Italian and even more excluded when they talk in English about England. I mean, Ascot. I haven't been to Ascot. Or shopped in Joseph in Knightsbridge. I'm out of my league here I thought, and I want to go back to my crumby hotel and crawl under the sheets. As the limo drove on, I couldn't stop staring at the girls as they chatted away. They eventually gave up on me and reverted back to their native tongue. They were everything, I thought I wanted to be. International women of sophistication and experience. I could never be like them, I thought. Not on the pocket money I get and this being my first time abroad.

As we drew nearer their hotel, we drove down a narrow street with a few shops and a restaurant where Arianna asked the driver to stop.

'Oh, do let's go in there,' she said. 'I read about it in *Harpers*. They have a new chef who is apparently the best in Florence. Everyone's talking about him. Are you hungry, Lucy? Want to give it a try?'

I was beginning to feel hungry, as I hadn't had a bite to eat all day and my food poisoning had pretty well disappeared. I nodded my head.

Arianna said something to the driver, then we got out of the car and made our way into the restaurant. It was very chic with a simple décor of white walls, abstract paintings in vibrant reds and purples, and flowers that looked like birds' heads on stems. The headwaiter came forward to greet the girls as if they were lifelong friends, took their coats and swept them away towards a white linen covered table. As an afterthought he came back and looked at me as if I had just crawled out from under a stone.

'Yes, I am with them,' I said and handed him my parka. I reminded myself of Nesta's favourite quote – no one can make you feel inferior without your permission. I was determined not to give my permission. OK, so I hadn't been to many places like this. Well, it's about time I started to, I thought.

Morsels of tasty bites arrived one after the other on enormous white plates. Each course was beautifully arranged as though there was an artist in the kitchen arranging each leaf, and it almost felt a shame to ruin the design. All of it tasted delicious and, although I hadn't got a clue what I was eating, I did my best to join in and enthuse with the girls and Teddy.

After lunch, I still felt hungry as the portions had been tiny and I found myself hankering for a cheeseburger and chips. I must be feeling a lot better, I thought as Teddy asked for the bill, then went off to find the driver.

Arianna got out her wallet so I followed her lead and pulled out my little Chinese purse.

'How much?' I asked.

She looked surprised. 'It's OK. I can pay. You are our guest.'

'No, no,' I insisted. 'Let's split it.' I didn't want her to think that I was hanging around with Teddy because he was rich or anything.

She looked at the bill. 'OK. This should cover our share,' she said as she put down a wad of euros. 'Now I must go and visit, as you say in English, the Ladies.'

Cecilia got up to join her. 'See you in a mo,' she said with a smile.

I smiled back. These girls were OK and really making an effort to be friendly, although I had noticed Cecilia eyeing up Teddy a few times and hanging on his every word. Clearly she doesn't see me as competition, I thought. She probably thinks that Teddy is hanging out with me because there was no one else around. I wonder if they're talking about me in the Ladies, asking each other what on earth Teddy's doing with a scruff-pot like me?

I picked up the bill to work out my share. One hundred and sixteen euros. A quarter of that would be? Ohmigod. I felt my heart sink. Twenty-nine euros. If only I hadn't bought so many of those mad *David* aprons. I only had twenty-five euros left and I still had to pay for my share of the chocolate the girls and I had eaten from the minibar.

As I was counting out my money, Teddy came back and pulled out his wallet. 'Here let me get that. You're my guest.'

I put my purse away, but I felt mortified.

I felt doubly bad as Arianna and Cecilia came back and witnessed Teddy paying my share of the bill as well as his, but neither of them said anything.

Best Thing for Food Poisoning

Drink plenty of fluid. Rest. Don't eat anything until the stomach settles and then eat only light food for a day or so. *Dr Watts*

Rest. Drink fluids. Have cheeseburger and chips, not posh titbits that cost a fortune. *Lucy*

Chapter 14

Cinderella

'Wow, get you,' said Nesta as I got out of the limo in front of the hotel. 'You won't be speaking to the likes of us mere mortals soon.'

The school bus had arrived back at the same time and everyone was getting off. Mrs Elwes looked surprised to see me up and about, so I quickly thanked my driver and hotfooted it back to the room with the girls before she did an inquisition and I found myself in trouble.

'Oh yes I will,' I said. 'Especially after the day I've had.' I'd never been happier to see my mates. People who understood me. Dressed like me. Spoke like me. Liked me. Not that Arianna and Cecilia didn't like me but, as the afternoon had gone on, I felt more and more inadequate. They'd insisted that I went back to the hotel with them after lunch and hang out. As it was my last day, I'd just wanted to be alone with Teddy, but he had some errands to run for his dad and so had to take off for a few hours.

He wouldn't hear of me going back to my hotel until the others were back so, in the end, I had no choice but to stay with the stepsisters. I suppose it did make sense in one way, I mean, why hang out in a drab hotel when you can luxuriate in beautiful surroundings. I just wished I'd felt more at home there.

As they'd unpacked cases of the most stunning clothes, Prada, Gucci, Fiorucci, they discussed a concert with some famous Italian rock band that they had tickets for that evening. As they'd said about the restaurant, anyone who was anyone was going to be there. Teddy included. I wondered why he hadn't mentioned it. Maybe now Arianna and Cecilia had arrived he wanted to hang out with them and, like most of Florence, I was history. 'Oh you'll be able to get a ticket from your concierge,' Arianna had said.

Not likely, I'd thought as I pictured the miserable being that inhabited reception at our hotel. We can't even get a glass of water from him. I wasn't bothered about going to a concert. I had hoped that Teddy might come over to my hotel like on the other evenings, but he phoned late afternoon and said that he wouldn't be back at all as he had something he had to do and would arrange for the car to drop me off. He didn't say anything about the evening. End of story, I thought. So much for my holiday romance. He wasn't even coming back to Hotel Corelli to say goodbye. Now that the girls had arrived maybe he'd realised that I didn't belong in his world. I'd served my purpose and was no longer needed.

'Rubbish,' said Nesta after I'd filled her, TJ and Izzie in.

'Yeah,' said Izzie. 'You're Cinderella, they're the ugly sisters and you shall go to the ball.'

'Ugly is one thing they're not,' I said. 'Believe me. They are geogorgeous with a capital G. And they were nice. Genuinely. So polite and . . .'

'I bet they have spotty bottoms,' interrupted Nesta.

'And bad breath,' said Izzie.

'And three nipples each,' said TJ. 'In fact, they sound so perfect, I bet that they're robots.'

I laughed. It was mad that I'd allowed myself to get so intimidated. I wouldn't have done if TJ, Nesta and Izzie had been with me.

'I want to go to the concert,' said Nesta. 'Everyone was talking about it on the bus and Mrs Elwes and Mr Johnson seemed cool about our lot going too. Liam and Jay got tickets on the internet before they came out here and Professor Snape, their teacher, is going too with a load of other boys from their school. Mrs Elwes said that if Snape was going, then we could go, as long as we stayed in a group. So . . . all we need are some tickets.'

'We need an insider,' said TJ. 'Some Italian who knows where we might get some.'

Nesta's face lit up. 'I know just the man. I'm going to go and ask Marco if he knows anything about it. I saw him go into the dining room when we got off the bus.'

She disappeared out of the door and, while she was gone, TJ and Izzie filled me in on their day out. It sounded like they'd had a great time and I wished I'd been with them, where I belonged, instead of feeling like an outsider in the Hotel Corelli.

Nesta returned fifteen minutes later looking flushed and happy. 'He spoke to me. At least, I spoke to him. He doesn't speak much English. God he's *so* gorgeous . . . Italian boys are so hot. He has the most amazing brown eyes . . .'

'Tickets, Nesta?' interrupted Izzie. 'Can he get us any?'

'Oh. Yes. He's playing with one of the warm-up bands tonight so he's got some complimentary ones.' She fished about in her pockets and produced tickets. 'So we can go. He's almost finished his shift and then his band are coming to pick him up. He said we could go with them and squeeze in the back of the van with the equipment. Not exactly a flash limo like you're used to, Lucy, but us lesser beings have to bum it sometimes.'

I thought I detected a note of sarcasm in Nesta's voice. I couldn't bear to think that they might have felt left out because I'd been swanning about in a limo and going to posh places. The last thing I needed was to be made to feel excluded by my best friends. 'You *know* it's not been like that, Nesta. I'd much rather have been with you today and I don't mind going in the back of a van. You know I don't.'

'Er, yes. But . . . um, one small problem . . . Marco only had three tickets.'

Izzie and TJ looked at each other, then at me.

'Well you obviously have to go, Nesta,' I said. 'You got the tickets and you like Marco.'

'Maybe we could all go and get all of us in,' she said. 'Maybe we could get tickets on the door.'

I shook my head. 'Doubt it. Arianna said it's been sold out for weeks. No. You guys all go. I'll stay here.'

'No,' said TJ. 'You can't do that. Nesta, you go on your own.'

'Noooo. Please. In a van with a load of strange boys? I might be mad, but I'm not that stupid. Oh come on, I can't go on my own. One of you come at least. Maybe we should put names in a hat or something.'

'We don't need to do that. I can stay with Lucy,' said Izzie. 'TJ, you go with Nesta.'

'No honestly,' I said. 'You three go. I'm really not bothered about going. Not now. I might see Teddy and the girls there and I've had enough humiliation for one day, thank you very much. It would be awful to go and see him there and he'd get all embarrassed because he'd know he didn't mention the gig to me. I'd hate to end the holiday on a sour note. So no. You go.' I held my nose up and tried to do what Nesta does when she's being melodramatic and trying to be noble. 'No. I shall stay here alone with my memories. With my broken heart and broken dreams . . .'

It took a bit more persuading but, in the end, the girls gave in and agreed to go. The room became a flurry of activity with hairdryers, make-up, clothes and shoes scattered all over the place as they got ready. Half an hour later, they looked fabulous. Maybe not decked out in Prada, but I reckoned they could give Arianna and Cecilia a run for their money.

'You sure you're going to be OK?' asked Nesta as she put her coat on ready for the off.

'Totally,' I said. 'I'll walk you out.'

At the back of the hotel, the van was in the car park where Marco had said it would be. The girls piled into the back with the other band members whose faces lit up when they saw that three stunning young girls were travelling with them.

'Now don't stay out too late,' I said, putting on my croaky old grandma voice. 'Don't take any drugs. And TJ, don't go licking strangers' ears. We know what you can be like when you're allowed out.'

'OK, Ma,' said TJ, laughing. 'Now you go get some cocoa and get back to your knitting.'

'Okee dokee,' I replied, trying to look as cheerful as possible.

After I'd waved them off, I went back to my room and lay on the bottom bunk. I couldn't help but feel low. Sometimes I don't feel that I belong anywhere, I thought as I flicked on the TV. I don't like it here in this crumby hotel and yet I felt uncomfortable at the Grand Hotel Villa Corelli. Where do I belong? I wish Tony was here, I thought. He'd make me laugh and get me out of this weird mood. Maybe my period's due and that's why I'm feeling emotional. Still, at least I know it is due. If I'd had sex with Tony, I might be here wondering if it was going to come at all. I wondered what Tony was doing over in England. If he'd gone to the rave and slept with Andrea Morton. I felt tears sting the back of my eyes. So much for me wanting to be a grown-up, a woman of experience and sophistication, I thought. I've never felt so young and so inexperienced in all my life. Pathetic. My one try at getting over Tony has turned out to be a disaster. My first holiday romance and here I am on the last night on my own. Dumped the moment Teddy got a better offer. How humiliating. I might try and kid myself that I can wing it in the world of grown-ups, but all those people in the past who've said 'You're not old enough', maybe, just maybe, they were right.

Just at that moment, I heard a rustling sound at the bottom of the door and saw an envelope being pushed through. As I got up to see what it was, I felt a stab of anticipation. Maybe it was a note from Teddy. It had my name on it, so I ripped open the envelope and went over to the lamp so that I could see better. Inside was a condom and a note, saying: *For a night to remember, my room, Number 14. 8.30. Chris.*

OK, Chris, I thought. Yeah. I'll give you night to remember.

'I thought you might take up my offer,' he said with a smirk when he opened his door five minutes later.

'Did you?' I said, putting on my most alluring smile. 'Yeah. How could I refuse an offer like that? But . . . I thought you might need a bit of cooling down first.' I produced the condom from behind my back. I'd filled it from the taps to make it into a water bomb so I bashed him over the head with it. 'But you know the awful thing about condoms? Well, they can burst.'

Water dripped down his face as it burst over his head. 'Your loss, you . . . you're so . . . childish,' he moaned as he ran back into his room. 'Anyway, you're . . . you're probably too young for me.'

Story of my life, mate, I thought as I made my way back to my room. Why fight it? I asked myself. Anyway, sometimes it's fun to act childish. Trying to be grown-up and mature, it stinks.

I lay back on the bed and giggled to myself. Yeah, condoms, they make brilliant water bombs. I must tell the girls when they come back. A moment later, the phone rang.

'I suppose you think you're *so* clever,' said Chris's voice.

'Well medium clever,' I replied. 'I don't like to boast.'

'You ought to grow up and act your age . . .'

'So you said. Don't you have anything new to say?'

'Just that I think you're a lesbian.'

'Oh. OK. Cool.' I said and put the phone down.

A moment later, the phone went again.

'Look, give me a break will you?' I said into the receiver. 'Just bog off and leave me alone. I don't fancy you. I never will and you can take your stupid condoms and stick them up your bum.'

'*Lucy* Lovering,' said Mr Johnson's voice. 'Who on *earth* do you think you're talking to?'

'Oh! Er . . . well, not you,' I gasped. 'Sorry sorry, oh God . . .'

'The dining room is about to close for supper,' he said in a clipped voice. 'If you're eating, you'll need to be there in five minutes.'

'Yes, Mr Johnson. Sorry, Mr Johnson.' Oh bugger, Mr Johnson, I thought as I put the phone down.

And then the phone went again.

'Hello . . .' I said cautiously.

'Hey Lucy,' said Teddy's voice. 'Phew. I thought I'd missed you.'

'Oh Teddy. Missed me? How? Why?'

'I tried your room about ten minutes ago, but no one picked up. Then it was engaged when I tried again. What are you doing?'

'Oh, going to have supper in a minute, then this and that. There's a whole crowd of us here, yeah, having a great time . . .' I was determined not to give away how much he'd hurt me. 'Why? What are you doing?' As if I didn't know, I thought.

'I was going to go to the concert.'

'Yeah, Arianna told me about it,' I said breezily. 'Well. Have a good time, must dash. It was nice meeting you.'

'Nice meeting me? Hey Lucy. Are you OK? You sound a bit weirded out.'

'No. I'm fine,' I said. 'Absolutely fine. Couldn't be better. Anyway, got to go now. Got a million things to do. Leaving tomorrow. So. Yeah. Have a great time at the concert.'

'Oh,' he said and I could hear disappointment in just that one word. 'Yeah. OK. Shame. See, I got you a ticket. That was why I couldn't get back to the Hotel Corelli to see you. I didn't want to say anything and get your hopes up in case I couldn't get one for you, but I managed it. Last one I think. But . . .'

'You got me a ticket?'

'Yeah.'

'But aren't you going with Arianna and Cecilia?'

'They're making their own way. Meeting a bunch of mates there. And just between you and me, I can only take so much of all their girlie stuff. It gets a bit boring after a while. It's like they can only ever talk about clothes and who's the latest in-person. I'd much rather have gone with you. At least I can have a decent conversation with you.'

I started to laugh. 'Is that all?'

'I think you know very well that's not all . . . but you know what I mean. Oh come on, you're going back to England tomorrow. We *can't* not spend our last night together. Who knows when we'll see each other again. Just . . . please, Lucy . . . I . . . I've never met anyone like you before. I really like you. You're different . . .'

'Like good or bad different?'

'Good. *Really* good, really, really . . .'

'I will come,' I interrupted.

'You *will*? Oh fantastic. I was so disappointed when I couldn't hang out with you today, but it was really hard getting that ticket. I had to go all over the place. I'll come and get you. Half an hour?'

Cinderella shall go to the ball, I thought when I put the phone down. Then I panicked. I had nothing to wear. I'd lent Izzie the only decent top I'd brought with me and all that was left were T-shirts I'd worn in the week. Oh God. I had half an hour. What was I going to wear? If I was Cinderella, wasn't my fairy godmother supposed to appear with the perfect dress? So where was she?

I opened the wardrobe but, nope, no fairy godmother in there or perfect dress. All I could see was a pile of dirty laundry.

I pulled out my black jeans. They would be OK if only I had something to wear with them. But what? I stared round the room looking for inspiration. Some of the girls' clothes were still scattered over the beds, but there was nothing there that fitted me. Izzie, Nesta and TJ are all so tall. With breasts. So what? Maybe I could do a Julie Andrews from *The Sound of Music* and make something out of the curtains. I'd brought my sewing kit with me. Mad idea, I thought. The curtains looked even dirtier than our laundry. So what? What? Arianna and Cecilia will probably be decked out in some fabulous little designer numbers, and Izzie, Nesta and TJ had all left looking like rock chicks. I don't want to turn up looking like some boring loser. I'm a designer, I thought. If I was at home, I could knock something up in a moment. There must be something I can use. I went back to the wardrobe and pulled out what was in there to see if anything could be adapted. T-shirts. More T-shirts. A frumpy old woolly. Couple of fleeces. Bags with assorted souvenirs in. The aprons with David's naked torso on them that we'd bought in the market up at Piazza Michelangelo. Yeah, Teddy would definitely think I was different if I turned up in one of those.

Then I had an idea.

I could make this work, I thought as I pulled an apron out of the bag and held it up against me. OK, so it might not be Prada or Versace, but they're not my style anyway. I might not have a fortune to spend on clothes, but I do have ideas. If I go to the ball, I want to go in a Lucy Lovering one-off creation.

How to Make a Water Bomb

Take either a balloon or a condom. Fill with cold water. Tie the end. *Voilà*. Bombs away!

Chapter 15

Concert

A spray of perfume, a last slick of lip-gloss and I pulled on my parka and went out to the reception to wait for Teddy.

'Off to the ball?' asked Mrs Elwes, appearing from the dining area and carrying a large glass of red wine.

I nodded. 'That American boy, Teddy, he got me a ticket. And we're meeting the others there.'

Mrs Elwes smiled. 'So what have you got on under there?'

'Um, top, jeans, the usual,' I said, then looked down at my sneakers. 'Shame about the shoes though. I didn't bring any glam ones as I knew we were going to be walking so much.'

'What size are you, Lucy?'

'Thirty-four. Why?'

'Give me a tic,' she said and ran off to her room. She was back minutes later with a large carrier bag. 'Somebody left these on the bus. I've been round everyone in our group and Nesta said they weren't yours. I think someone from the last school trip must have left them.'

She produced a pair of shoes from the box and I gasped. They were perfect. Black, high and strappy.

'But won't someone write to reception and ask for them?' I asked.

Mrs Elwes took a sip of her wine. 'Huh. I tried handing them in. The concierge just looked at me, waved me away and said, "No polish, no polish" . . . I give up with that man. He's been completely unhelpful since day one.'

I looked at the shoes. 'Can I really?'

Mrs Elwes smiled again. I think she was feeling a little happy from the wine. 'Sure, go ahead,' she said.

I quickly pulled off my trainers and stepped into the shoes. They fitted perfectly.

'Cool,' said Mrs Elwes.

I felt like hugging her. 'Anyone ever tell you you were their fairy godmother before?'

'That's me. Cinderella you shall go to the ball,' said Mrs Elwes. She waved an imaginary wand, then tottered off towards the lounge.

Five minutes later, my carriage arrived and I was on the way to the ball, er . . . rock concert. Teddy was so sweet on the journey and held my hand all the way. We didn't say much and I felt a stab of sadness as I watched the lights of Florence flash by outside the window. This was our last night together and maybe I'd never see him again. I got the feeling that he was thinking the same thing.

The concert was being held in an old hall on the edge of town and already there were crowds waiting outside when we arrived. They all stopped and stared when the limo pulled up.

'Who is it, who is it?' I heard a few of them ask.

Someone in the crowd said, 'Nobody,' in a disappointed tone. I laughed as Teddy handed our tickets to one of the men on the door and we were ushered through.

'I'm going to leave my coat in the cloakroom, then see if I can find my mates,' I said.

'And I'll look for Arianna and Co,' said Teddy. 'Meet you back here in five minutes?'

I nodded and went to the cloakroom to get rid of my parka. I felt a brief pang of nerves as I discarded the jacket and hoped that I hadn't made a huge mistake in my outfit.

'*Da paura, il tuo* top,' said the girl behind the desk.

I looked at her quizzically and shrugged. 'English, no understand.'

She smiled, looked me up and down, then gave me the thumbs up. Maybe my top would be OK after all.

'Lucy,' a voice called behind me. I turned, and there were Izzie and TJ making their way towards me through the people swarming inside the main hall.

'Wow,' said TJ and pointed at my top. 'Where did you get that?'

'Er . . . it's a Lucy Lovering special. Do you like it?'

'It's brilliant,' said TJ. 'I want one.'

I'd cut the bottom of the apron, hemmed the top, then cut

the black ties off three more of the aprons and I'd quickly sewn on six hooks so that the ties could be laced up my back. When I put it on I had the perfect halter handkerchief top with black straps at the back.

'But the choker,' said Izzie. 'That's gorgeous. I've never seen that before.'

I grinned. 'Oh yes you have. It was Velcroed round the lamp in our room, remember. I'll stick it back later.'

The choker was my last moment of inspiration. The lamp was the only half-decent thing in our room, red with a red velvet fringe from which dripped red beads. It made the perfect choker when I took it off and tied it round my neck.

'Lucy, you're a genius,' said Izzie. 'And will you make me one of those tops too when we get back?'

'Sure,' I said. 'Only we need to get down the market before our flight tomorrow and buy up some supplies, and I . . . I'm sorry, but I cut the straps off three of the aprons.'

'No worries,' said TJ. 'They didn't cost much and anyway, we can easily sew them back on.'

Teddy appeared a moment later with his stepsisters. He gave me a long appreciative look up and down and I felt myself blushing.

'Lucy,' said Arianna as she came over to me and gave me the two-cheek kiss. 'You look fab. Who's it by?'

'It's an original,' I said. 'An LL creation made specially for me.'

'LL,' she said. 'Yeah. I think I've heard of them.'

'She made it herself,' said TJ. 'She's LL.'

Arianna looked well impressed.

'It's so cool – Italian and cheeky at the same time,' gushed Cecilia. 'Oh please could you make two, for Arianna and me.'

'Sure,' I said. 'And these are my friends, Izzie and TJ. Hey, where's Nesta?'

'Oh somewhere draped all over Marco,' said Izzie. 'I think he finally gave in.'

'I knew it was only a matter of time,' I said.

After that, the evening was great. The bands were wild and the music even wilder. It felt brilliant to be bopping away, even though I didn't understand a word that anyone was singing. And my *David* top went down a storm. By the end of the evening, I had twelve orders from girls at our school, plus the two from Arianna and Cecilia. So much for it being a one-off original, I thought.

'LL Designs branch out to Italy,' said Nesta, when she took a moment to detach herself from Marco. 'I think we should go into business.'

'Yeah,' said TJ. 'Lucy can make them. I'll do the advertising, Nesta can model them . . .'

'And I'll sing about them,' grinned Izzie. 'Oh cor blimey, very rum, the statue of *David*'s lost his bum . . . Hhhm. Maybe not. OK, I'll work on the lyrics.'

Teddy offered to give us all a lift home after the gig and we had to drag Nesta away from Marco. She was in tears when she got into the car.

'He promised he'll write, but I know he won't,' she sobbed.

'It's too sad . . . I meet the love of my life and we're destined to part . . .'

'Love of your life?' asked Izzie. 'Hey come on, you've hardly said two words to each other as he doesn't speak good English.'

'But I speak some Italian. Anyway, we don't need words. We speak the language of love,' she said and looked wistfully out of the window.

Teddy glanced over at me and gave me a sad smile. I wonder if you are going to make false promises to write, I thought. Or if we'll ever meet again.

When we got back to the hotel, the girls very sensitively made themselves scarce and left Teddy and me alone. We walked around the car park, then went and sat on a wall at the back where Teddy pulled me close to him.

'Guess this is it, then, Lucy Lovering Junior,' he said as he tucked a strand of hair behind my ear.

'Guess so, Teddy Junior.'

He leaned forward and gave me a long, lovely kiss, then he pulled back.

'I will write if you'd like,' he said. 'I know I want to stay in touch. We can e-mail. And I can send you photos from back home.'

I nodded. 'I'd like that. And, with the profits of my *David* tops, the first thing I'm going to buy is a digital camera so I can send you photos too.'

'Cool. I'd really like to see where you live and your family and all. And send me pics of some more of your designs. I'd really love to see them if tonight's creation is anything to go by.'

'I will. And send me some of your designs. I'd really like to see them too.'

And then there didn't seem to be anything else to say. We kissed a little longer, but we both knew that at some time we had to part. I walked him back to his car and we held each other for a few moments. Then he got in and gave the driver the nod. I felt so sad as I watched the car start up, then make its way out of the car park, on to the street and out of my life.

How to Make an LL Handkerchief Top Out of an Apron

Cut off the part of the apron that would hang below the waist.

Put on the top part and measure how long you want the top to be (i.e. to the top of your jeans or, if you have a fab midriff, cut to a few inches under your bust).

Sew four or six loops on to the side of the apron front. Two at the bust, two at the bottom (and, if you want more lacing at the back, two in between the bust and bottom).

Cut off the straps that would have gone round your waist and use them to lace in a criss-cross across your back.

If you have any strap left, use it to edge the hem for a neat finish. If not, sew a hem on the bottom so that you have a neat line.

And there's your top. If you lace it tight, it will look really cool.

Chapter 16

Homeward Bound

'I can't wait to see Mojo,' said TJ as she strapped herself into her seat belt ready for the flight back to London. 'I've missed him like mad.'

I felt a stab of guilt. I hadn't thought about our dogs, not once. And I'd hardly thought about my family at all. There had been too much going on. But now we were settled on the plane and our goodbyes had been said, I realised that I was looking forward to going home. Back to my own bed. Peanut butter and honey on toast for breakfast and a decent cup of tea. Soon Florence and Teddy would be a distant dream, and London my reality once more. I wondered how things would have been if I'd met Teddy in my everyday life. Had it felt so special because of where we were? No, it wasn't only the location, I decided. We'd have got on wherever we were. He was a genuinely nice guy. But back to normal, back to school. Ugh. And Tony.

Hhmm. I wasn't sure how I felt about that. The school trip had been the perfect distraction from him, but now I was going back and I'd have to face him sooner or later round at Nesta's.

'You feeling OK this time?' asked TJ, as the plane started up its engines and we began to cruise down the runway ready for take-off.

I nodded. I did feel fine. Completely different to the journey out. I felt calm. I'd done it before. Maybe there were some aspects of my life where I had become a woman of experience.

Everyone seemed quiet as we took off. Girls were staring out of the windows, each of us lost in our private memories of Florence.

It didn't last long. As soon as we were up in the sky and the seat-belt sign had been switched off, people started swapping places, girls going to sit with the boys, boys chatting up the girls, the teachers looking weary and glad it was all almost over.

'Life goes on,' I said to TJ. 'And time waits for no man . . . or woman or something like that.'

She laughed. 'Feeling philosophical, are we?'

'Sort of.'

'You OK about leaving Teddy?'

I nodded. 'Sort of. Yeah. No choice had I?' I had felt a little sad, but was fine about it in the end. He'd rung our hotel early this morning and asked if he could see me off at the airport. I'd told him no. For one thing, it would have been awkward having everyone there and staring at us, and we wouldn't have been able to snog properly, not under the eagle eye of Mrs Elwes and

Mr Johnson, who was now, according to some sources, back on twenty cigarettes a day. I wanted to remember the concert as our last time together and Teddy had understood. He'd also promised to come over to England sometime. And I'd promised I'd go to visit him in the States when I was older. I really meant it too. I had the feeling that Teddy and I would be friends for a long time.

About an hour into the flight, an announcement came on asking everyone to return to their seats and fasten their belts.

'Why's that?' I asked TJ. 'We're not landing yet.'

'Probably going to run into some turbulence,' she said. 'It happens all the time. Nothing to worry a . . . a woaaaaaah . . .'

A sudden lurch and it felt like the plane was falling out of the sky. A scream went through the back of the cabin. Mainly from the girls from our school. And Liam.

'You OK?' asked TJ, clinging on to the seat rest as the plane steadied itself. 'It will probably only last a minute or so.'

The plane took what felt like another dive and books and magazines went flying. 'Er . . . yeah.'

Only the turbulence didn't last a minute. It went on and on, as if the plane had suddenly been put in a washing machine. On spin. Bump bump theewump. My new-found calm disappeared as a voice in my head said, ohmigod, we're gonna diiiiiieeeeeeeee.

I wasn't the only one who looked freaked. Liam, who was sitting in the middle aisle opposite TJ and me, threw up all over Chris who was next to him.

'Eeew,' cried Nesta. 'Gross.' She'd never make a good nurse, I thought as Liam turned greener and greener. A flight attendant attempted to clean him up, but she was swaying all over the place and eventually gave up, reassuring him that she'd be back in a minute.

'Hold hands, hold hands,' said Izzie from the seat behind. She and Nesta leaned forward and TJ and I leaned back and we joined hands over the tops of our seats.

'It's g . . . g . . . going to be OK,' said Nesta. 'Just a storm or something.'

'Oh *no,*' moaned Izzie, as the plane lurched up, down and sideways. 'That means lightning and that means it might hit the plane.'

'Oh thanks a *lot,*' I said. 'But, look, you guys, I just want you to know that you're the best friends I've ever had and I really, *really* love you.'

'And I want you to know that I really, *really* love you as well,' said Nesta.

'Try meditating,' said Izzie as she took a deep breath. 'It will help calm us down.'

'No way,' said Nesta. 'If I'm going to die, I'm not spending my last moments chanting om shanti wotnot or whatever.'

'Then what do you suggest?' asked Izzie.

'Praying. Begging. I dunno.'

'Let's sing,' said TJ. 'Hmmm. Let me think. Songs for plane crashes . . . Hhmmm. *Ah ah ah ah, Staying Alive . . .*'

'Hhhm, good choice, TJ,' said Izzie.

'We're not going to die,' I said. 'And we're not going to crash.

Cut it out, TJ. You said it would only last a few minutes.'

'I lied,' said TJ, who by now was almost as green as Liam. 'Sometimes it can go on for ages.'

I shut my eyes tight and, as the plane rattled and bounced along, I prayed that we'd make it home. Please, please God, let me see my mum and dad one more time. And Steve and Lal. And . . . and Tony. I wanted to see Tony one last time. Oh God. I really, really did. So we might have had fallings-out, but now, when it came to the crunch, it was his face I saw in my mind, not the lovely Teddy. We'd been through so much together. Oh God, oh God, I thought. I'll be ever so good if you get us through this and I promise I won't only pray at exam times or when I'm travelling. I promise, God. I'll pray in between when everything's all right.

As suddenly as it had started, the turbulence ended and everyone breathed a huge sigh of relief. An announcement came over the intercom that we were through the bad weather and it was going to be plain sailing from then on. Only we're flying, I thought, then looked out the window just to check that the pilot hadn't actually been correct and we'd landed in the sea and were plain sailing. Or a plane sailing. But no, fluffy clouds were all that I could see.

'I still mean it that I love you guys,' I said.

'Ditto,' said Nesta. 'Now where's our lunch?'

That's one thing I love about Nesta. She can go down fast, but she can come up even quicker.

The rest of the flight went smoothly and, before we knew it, we were starting to descend into London. It was grey and cold as we got off the plane, but it did feel good to be back on solid ground and not thirty-five thousand feet up in the air being thrown about. We were through Passport Control quickly enough, then it was off to collect our luggage before getting on to the coach for the last leg of the journey back to school where Mum or Dad would be waiting. Well, hello London, I thought as we walked through Customs and through the arrival gates. Crowds of people were waiting behind the barriers for friends and relatives, some with names on cardboard, one family with a banner saying, 'Welcome home'. It felt nice and festive watching all the eager faces waiting to greet their loved ones. And it felt good to be able to understand everything that was being said all around us again.

'*It's nice to go travelling,*' sang Mr Johnson as he wheeled his trolley past us, '*in winter, summer or rain, but it's so much nicer, yes it's so much nicer to come home.*'

Izzie laughed and nudged me. 'He seems happy,' she said with a grin.

'I wonder why,' I said. 'I mean, most men would be happy to go away with twenty-five gorgeous young girls.'

'Ah . . . look,' said Izzie, pointing to the end of the line of people waiting for arrivals. 'So sweet.'

I glanced to where she was pointing and there was a boy dressed in jeans and a black coat. I couldn't see his face as it was partly obscured by the most enormous bunch of white roses. How romantic, I thought. He's come to meet his girlfriend and, judging by the size of that stunning bouquet, she means a lot to him.

'Oh. My. God,' said TJ, then nudged me. I turned to look at her and saw that her face registered surprise. She pointed at the boy with the flowers again.

I looked back at him.

Now I could see his face.

It was Tony.